To Stacy, Barry, & L.C.

Crystalline

An Illustrated Novel

✳

Robert Maisano

[signature]

Biplane Media   Seattle, Washington

Biplane Media
415 1st Avenue North, Suite 9555 Seattle, WA 98109
www.biplane.media

Library of Congress Cataloging-in-Publication Data

Names: Maisano, Robert, 1991– author.
Title: Crystalline : an illustrated novel
Description: First Edition. | Seattle : Biplane Media, 2019.
Identifiers: LCCN 2019900127 |ISBN 978-0-9994195-3-3 (hardcover) |
ISBN 978-0-9994195-4-0 (ebook)
LC record available at https://lccn.loc.gov/2019900127
p. cm.

All artwork by Beeple. Additional information on the artist, environmental sustainability notes, citations, and additional credits are located at the back of the book in the Acknowledgement section.

Printed in the United States.

10 9 8 7 6 5 4 3 2 1

A note about ebook formatting: the imagery and text may vary in this medium as it needs to be versatile enough to accommodate different devices.

For Ashley Rose, the star I steer by.

PREFACE

The remarkable thing about science fiction is that it seldom remains fiction. Cellphones, computers, spaceships, MRIs, VR headsets, 3D printers; it's an endless list of what were once mere ideas. Now, they're not only reality but affecting our everyday lives. The second thing to remember is the creator of the idea isn't typically the one who brings into reality. It's the readers that are hit with the same spark of inspiration. Paul Allen, Steve Jobs, Jeff Bezos, Elon Musk all grew up reading science fiction. SpaceX's rockets are inspiration from Elon Musk reading the *Tintin Destination Moon* series. Not only in mirroring the vertical takeoff and landing capability but also design. "I love the Tintin rocket design, so I kind of wanted to bias it toward that."[†] This is why I write.

I write because I cannot turn my mind off. It's a burden at times. I've torn the labels off of ketchup bottles to write. The idea stream is like a never-ending waterfall: powerful, ceaseless, nourishing. I write science fiction because it's important to hone these ideas and stories. A crazy product idea is just that, an idea to riff about amongst friends at the bar. But taking a *what if* scenario and shaping that into a 200-page book means you have to look at the idea from all angles. You must breathe life into the damn thing. I picture these stories like one long cipher and I'm the one who has to uncover the message. Then I must make it interesting enough for *you* to stay with me throughout the whole tale.

Additionally, I feel as we get older our view of what's possible decays like an atrophied muscle. Practicality and cynicism are malignancies adults only discover after it's too late. Keeping wonder alive, allowing your mind to travel, entertain, and empathize, is what keeps us healthy. It doesn't stop there. Stories can warm your heart for years after closing the book. There are books I can point to that have led to a thriving relationship with my fiancé and family. Humans don't learn by instruction, they learn by metaphor.

Science Fiction stories can also be critical warnings. Bradbury's *Fahrenheit 451* and Orwell's *1984* caution of demagoguery and the terror of following the masses. The film *Wall-E* shows the dangers of excess. Carl Sagan's *Contact* and Kim Stanley Robinson's *Aurora* display the importance of why humankind should seek peace in order to prolong our existence on Earth. All brilliant stories with unforgettable messages.

The stories I write have warnings too. The speed at which social media has changed us is frightening. In under a decade our society has been turned around by the power of connection and isolation.[‡] Online dating, image-crafting, influencers, the gig economy, cyberbullying, has spread faster than a high-wind wildfire.

These are some of the issues that inspired this book you're holding. *Crystalline* began by asking "what if a social media company became so powerful it built a private city?" Tech companies, especially in Silicon Valley, have a utopian view on their creations. But they're almost always too grandiose. Which makes me wonder if there's malice behind what they're doing.[§] After all, these companies are selling your data to the highest bidders.

I should note this isn't an anti-capitalist or anti-tech book. It's a story about a future that could be ours one day. It is my hope that if we're ever at a crossroads in the future and it rhymes with this story, that we pause and reconsider what might this lead to. Finally, I wrote this to book to entertain. Some projects are painful to write, this one wasn't, it was enjoyable all the way through. The illustrations from the incredibly brilliant artist, Beeple, add a striking visual quality that cannot be found in any other book of its kind. Read on and enjoy the story of *Crystalline*.

Crystalline

ONE

Cole Wainwright looked over the walls of Crystalline and prayed his sister was still breathing. He hadn't heard from her in weeks. Cole, along with everyone outside Crystalline, wasn't allowed in. It was America's first city built entirely by a private company, the Janus Corporation. Being an employee isn't enough; the city only welcomes those who have and maintain top social network scores. *A self-proclaimed utopia that governs like a police-state*, Cole thought as he scanned the top of the walls with his binoculars. The pit in his stomach grew as he thought of his sister.

"Cole, what's the pressure readout?" a voice shouted from a radio.

"4,000 PSI," Cole replied to his crew below the command tower. "Look guys, I think it should be brought down to 3,000 PSI, you're straining the—"

"Don't worry 'bout it CalTech, we got it under control."

Cole rolled his eyes. "It's MIT," he didn't transmit into the radio. "Alright Rafiq, just remember that's the main water pipe and we can't afford a burst—"

"Yeah, yeah, yeah."

Cole threw the radio on the desk and continued to scan the skyline. Tall spires cut through morning fog like pins through cotton. Coordinated trails of green, blue, and yellow scurried around the buildings in a constant rhythm, drone traffic. Remnants of Neo Gothic buildings harkened to a time before Crystalline. The city before it was built in a boom era and was the first to fall when the economy went south, eventually going bankrupt. Cole continued to look across the pink neon skyline even though he had no idea where his sister, Ainsley, lived.

"What's it read now?" Rafiq asked. The construction equipment grew louder. Cole began to feel irritated.

"4,200 PSI, guys. I've run the calculations twice, that's too much pressure. If you divert the pipe to another system—"

"Eh, we got it."

The earth began to hum. Cole watched his coffee mug vibrate across the table. Rubbing his temples, he imagined himself in an office with software engineers, a place where he should be. He pushed the thought from his mind. Cole had been expelled from MIT and become a commercial plumber. There were few lucrative careers outside Crystalline. People had to take what they could get.

"Cole, I think you should get down here," Rafiq said, hiding shame.

Cole drank the rest of his coffee and hustled down the metal stairs that wrapped around the tower. He couldn't take his eyes off the skyline. "Where are you, Ainsley?" he said aloud to the foul air.

On the ground, his men were trying to tighten various valves against a gray stone wall. Black pipes with silver joints fed from the wall into the ground. Copper pipes ran parallel, glistening in the sunlight. The massive white pipe with blue joints gave Cole an uneasy feeling. He noticed the main line for the building was oscillating. Rafiq wiped sweat from his brow and approached Cole.

"You were right. 3,000 PSI would've been easier."

Cole didn't say anything. The vibrations grew stronger. Now a distant metal clang sounded.

"Did you try alleviating—"

"Get back! Pressure just spiked to 9,000 PSI," a nearby worker shouted. The white pipe began stirring like a hummingbird and the blue joints ruptured simultaneously. Water sprayed from the openings and soon the entire pipe split, shooting water and mud into the sky. It began raining down on the entire crew.

Rafiq wiped the mess off his face. "Welp, at least it wasn't a septic pipe," he said, smirking.

Cole, unamused, ordered him to shut down the system. This mishap would cost them dearly. Cole spent the rest of day cleaning up the mess of his colleagues until the sun bowed behind Crystalline, casting all the buildings in a wondrous translucent tint of amber and pink. Cole was the last to punch out and head home.

Inside his apartment, he stripped down and hurried to the shower, tossing the clothes and boots into the wash-pod on the way. Through the porthole window he could see Crystalline; the night skyline peppered with purple and red lights. The shapes of buildings glowed and shimmered as drone traffic buzzed above alleyways and boulevards. Hollow pain sank into Cole. He wished he was a Crystallean. They worked in clean offices and made a prosperous wage. The mistakes he made in college forever barred him from the city.

The comms tile beside the bathroom sink mirror lit up. Someone was calling him. "Dammit." Cole knew it was his parents calling. They had virtual dinners every Wednesday. Ainsley used to join but stopped once she married Martin Spiros. Imagine a Ken-doll but stupider. They moved to Crystalline together. Cole told the comms tile he needed five minutes.

The dinner went fast. Cole ate leftovers and looked across the table at his parents, who seemed to be grayer, but more spry than him. They lived happily in Colorado. Their lives were relatively tech-free, besides the virtual dinner tech that Cole bought them. There was no mention of Ainsley. Cole's parents always had the mindset of letting their children figure life out on their own. They didn't want to intervene. Cole thought it was a dispersion of responsibility but knew mentioning that would only lead to a fight.

After dinner, Cole emptied the food scraps into the trash, grabbed a Louis L'Amour paperback, and climbed into bed. By the third page he fell asleep. Cole found himself in a deep dream. He was running from something. Voices told him hurry, but he was stuck in a molasses-like fluid. He couldn't make it. Turning around he saw the pack of guards with screens on their faces surround him.

Cole stirred awake, breathing hard and sweating into the warm sheets. He noticed a strange yellow-green light emitting from the living room. Cole tried dismissing it, but then the light blinked. A moment later a small pinging sounded. It was low in tone, almost courteous, like a doorbell at an estate. Cole climbed out of bed, shivering now from the sweat, and opened the door to the living room. The light was coming from the window. A mailer drone stood hovering in front of the delivery hatch. "Do you have any idea what time it is?" Cole said, opening the hatch.

A quaint androgynous digital voice replied, "3:03 AM Central Time; face the camera please to confirm identity." The drone's light centered around Cole's face, blinding him for a moment. "Identity verified." An electric arm extended from the cargo pod holding an orange envelope.

"Who's this from?" Cole asked.

The drone remained silent.

Cole took hold of the envelope and the mechanical arm shot back into itself. "Thank you. Have a pleasant day," the drone said, and then it flew below into the depths of the city, its motors roaring. Cole shut the window and climbed back into his warm bed.

There wasn't a return address on the envelope. He opened it carefully, trying to recall the last time he received a paper letter. Once his grandparents died they stopped arriving. An antique polaroid photo slid out. The woman in the photo looked like Ainsley, but her face was purple and swollen. Written on the tag at the bottom gave Cole a sour feeling. *A.W.* His sister's initials. "What the hell is this?" Cole said aloud. He pulled out a slip of paper from the envelope. It felt cheaply laminated. Unfolding it, he noticed it was a map, but couldn't determine of where. The last thing from the envelope was a moldering business card. Half of the writing was in Chinese, but the street address looked to be nearby. *Woo Fong Apothecary.* He flipped it over and recognized Ainsley's handwriting. *C, get here now, call this number from Woo Fong's phone.* The number below didn't make any sense. It was a landline. Cole looked at the photo of his sister again. She was alive, but he didn't know for how long.

TWO

The Woo Fong Apothecary shop was in the center of Chinatown, a dangerous area of the city, full of vagrants. Cole walked fast through the district, stepping over needles and shell casings. The sun seemed to be stuck below the horizon. Frost lingered against car windows and barred doors. Somewhere a dog squealed in agony.

Cole's glasses directed him toward the shop. Small arrows projected on the street in an augmented guidance system. A graduation gift his parents got him, despite his early termination at university.

Steam rose from sewer grates and low-flying passenger cabs navigated above the dilapidated buildings. Most of them used shipping containers as accommodations for the growing populous. Cole shuddered. He was worried. *What the hell happened to Ainsley? Why the polaroid?* People only go analog when they are hiding something serious. The Crystalline Guard rule with an iron fist. If you're not following their high standards, your life can become very difficult, or at least that's the rumor Cole heard. The society was built around a perfect lifestyle to the point of pollyannaish insanity. The daily social content publicized looked flawless: healthy children, delicious meals set in picture-perfect form, exquisite homes, designer pets. Which explained the endless applications to the company that founded the city, Janus Corporation. A beaten face didn't fit the life of a Crystallean, and the Janus Corporation would do anything to prevent that image from going public.

The glasses lit up the storefront before him in green. *You have arrived* ran across the lenses as they powered down. To Cole's surprise it was open. Inside, a frail Chinese man with graying wisps of hair and thick glasses manned the cash register. He didn't even turn when Cole entered the cluttered shop. High shelves with jars of various elixirs and solutions towered to the ceiling. The narrow aisles made it feel like the entire shop was hugging him. A strong odor of garlic, cinnamon and cat urine lingered.

Cole approached the frail man and slid the card across the counter to him, pointing to the landline number. The man did not speak. He held up his hand, showing Cole his wrinkled palm.

"Five bucks?" Cole asked.

The man shook his head.

"Fifty?"

The man nodded.

Cole rolled his eyes and beamed his watch toward the man. The old cash register lit up briefly and pinged. The man pointed to a door at the back of the room. Cole hurried over, opened it and stepped inside. It was an even smaller annex with narrower aisles, more jars of indescribable murk lined the shelves. Medical equipment for the elderly, walkers, bedpans and crutches, were organized neatly in the far corner of the annex. Stepping over decaying newspapers, he looked around for a phone. At the back of the room he spotted a periwinkle blue rotary phone. Cole set the receiver against his ear and heard a dial tone, something he hasn't heard since he was kid. The slow sliding of the dial made him anxious. The tone ceased as the phone connected through archaic lines. An even-paced ringing took over, it rang and rang and rang until someone on the other end picked up.

"Cole?"

"Ainsley?" He could hear her sobbing.

"Yes. Good, my message went through."

"Ainsley, what's going on? What is all this about? Where have you been?"

"Listen, I'm okay, I just need to protect myself. Things have been getting worse over here. It's Martin…he…" Ainsley breathed into the receiver. "He's been doing this."

"Beating you?"

"Yes."

"Jesus, how long has this been going on?"

"Cole, I need help. I need to leave Crystalline."

Cole found this statement strange. "Why can't you just hop on a train and go?"

"It's not that simple." Ainsley paused. "You ever notice that Crystalleans aren't on your side of the wall?"

"Because we're the unwashed masses?"

"We can't leave, Cole. I've been trying to escape for the last year. The city is a prison. Under strict watch. And Martin works for the societal government, too."

Cole said nothing.

"I need you to get me out, Cole, I don't know how much longer I have left."

THREE

"Thirty-six hours, Cole. You need to get here before then. That's when they'll be back."

"Who? And how do you expect me to get over there?" Cole asked.

"I know you'll find a way. You always have." Ainsley proceeded to tell Cole about the map he was holding. Since she was married to a societal government member, she lived in Pylône Sept, one of the tallest towers in Crystalline, located at the edge of the Gaslamp District on the western side of the city. Cole studied the map. His mouth was dry and he could hear Ainsley's shuddering breath. "Shit. Cole, I have to go, someone's coming."

"Wait how will I—" The phone went dead. Cole stood in the dim apothecary annex and tried to think. He knew it wasn't impossible. He returned to the main room and passed by the frail man. "Ahem," the man said. He spoke gently.

"What?" Cole asked.

The man continued to speak, but not in English, and pointed to a vial beside Cole. It had a greenish tint, filled with a gel membrane. Cole examined it and noticed a severed finger was encased in it. Cole jumped back from the grotesque sight. The frail man chuckled. "Take. You need. You need."

"The hell is the matter with you?"

"Crystalline. You need. Take."

Cole stared at the man. He could feel his world turning upside-down and had a suspicious feeling this was only the beginning of something new and terrifying. Cole took the vial, left the Woo Fong Apothecary and stepped out into the damp morning. He couldn't shake the image of his sister: purple-faced, eyelid swollen shut, the fear in her voice. What he didn't understand was why this would happen inside America's first utopian city.

The city opened three decades after social media proliferated throughout the world. Each year these platforms were optimized to become more addictive. No longer was there downtime from them. Using the services became as ubiquitous as breathing air. Every interaction, event, meal, was shared on these platforms. The Janus Corporation captured every trace of available data and monetized it. They either crushed or absorbed their competitors. After they became the most valuable company in the world by a factor of ten, they decided to build their new headquarters away from Silicon Valley. It was hailed as a great social experiment, but soon took on a velocity no one could slow. Janus struck a deal with the State and Federal government to take over a bankrupt city and payoff the outstanding debts.

Janus employees, comprised primarily of engineers, formed a government to rule the new city. Since they were data czars, they formulated a way to allow new citizens inside. The first criteria: they must work for Janus Corporation. Then they referenced their aggregate record from all the social networks and evaluated it through various artificial intelligence software. The software was so powerful it could nearly predict what type of person someone will be with just two years of social network data. Will the person steal? Lie on their taxes? Cheat on their spouse? The software evaluated this. This raised a controversial issue. Of course no one wants murders in a city, but this software expanded into the less serious offenses. The governing body of Crystalline, known as the Societal Government, kept pushing forward. Within a year, people who had a record of sharing inappropriate videos or posting offensive jokes to friends were banned from the city.

"It is postmodern neo-corporatism gone awry," Cole once wrote in a post describing the new city when he was studying at MIT. This became one of the first marks against him. Then the MIT fiasco became a scarlet letter on his records.

The city continued to receive support and praise from the Federal government, Silicon Valley, and technical universities, the three sects of America where ideological and monetary interests were aligned perfectly. Janus Corporation's plan for Crystalline was simple: build America's first utopia and be the model of future cities. They already sent teams to other decaying cities in Texas, Illinois, the Dakotas and New England. Cole imagined Crystalline as a cancer cell ready to become malignant.

Cole returned to his apartment and spread out the map across his kitchen table. He stared at it, thinking of how to infiltrate Crystalline. One thing he knew for certain was that he'd need some help.

<u>FOUR</u>

The construction site where Cole worked stood empty in the morning light. Carnage from the previous day's pipe rupture had been cleaned up, though a faint odor lingered. A man muscled a wheelbarrow through the mud, tossing scrap into it. The man heaved steel pipes over his shoulder and laid them into the basket. Normally this was a job for three men, but he was different. His name was Duke, the foreman of the construction company, Cole's boss.

Duke, who had gray-temples and stood at nearly seven feet, tossed another pipe into the basket. He paused to wipe sweat from his brow, his massive chest breathing in and out, then he continued to work. A Goliath who walked the earth. Despite his rank on the team, he arrived before any employees. No job was beneath him. He lived by a set of unwavering principles, the first being: *Do honest work.*

An hour passed before Duke saw another worker show up: Cole. They gave each other a wave. Duke noticed the tray of coffees he brought and set the wheelbarrow down in the mud. "Which has no fuss in it?" Duke asked.

Cole pointed to the cup that had *Duke* written on it.

"Thanks," Duke grunted. The coffee cup looked like a shot glass in his hand.

They drank in silence for a long time, watching the drone traffic circle Crystalline in the distance. Flashes of white and green lights mixed in with the ascending heatwaves off the horizon. Duke appreciated the value Cole had for silence. Not many men his age knew this virtue yet. It might explain why Cole had yet to become friends with any of the other men. He was different. There was no hiding his intellect. Duke looked at Cole, who seemed a bit more nervous than usual.

"You good?" Duke asked.

"No. There's something I need to talk to you about, but I don't know where to begin,"

"First thought, best thought."

Cole took a swig of coffee and sighed. "I need you to help me break into Crystalline."

Duke didn't say anything.

Cole continued. "I've heard the guys saying they've gone over before and I know you have too." Cole motioned to a medallion Duke wore, a design of stainless steel and tritium radio-luminescence tubes made only inside the walls of Crystalline.

Duke nodded. "There's still something you're not telling me."

Cole stared at the glimmering skyline, now awash in daylight. "Ainsley, my sister, she's in trouble. She's hurt. I need to get her out of the city."

Duke spat. "So much for the pinnacle of civilization."

"She only has thirty-six hours."

"What happens after then?"

Cole looked at his feet. "I don't know, I don't know. You think you can help me convince the guys? I feel if it came from you—"

"How's she going to deal with being tagged?"

"Tagged?"

"Yeah, tell me she has a plan for that."

"What the hell is *tagged*?"

Duke's eyebrows raised. "Shit kid, you got a lot to learn about that place. Every Crystallean has an RFID chip embedded under their skin, usually their left hand. It was sold as a convenience item at first, giving them the ability to pay faster, unlock their cars and homes, that kind of stuff."

Cole ran his hands through his hair. "Okay, that's a detail she left out."

Duke chuckled. "You know more about computers than anyone. I'm sure she knows you'll figure it out."

Cole raised his cup to drink but a rock knocked it out of his hands. It fell to the ground and spilled out into the dirt. He glanced over and saw Rafiq laughing. "Ba-boom! Ten points," Rafiq called out. Duke smirked. It was an impressive shot.

"No coffee for you, Rafiq," Cole said, taking his cup.

"Ah c'mon, how am I going to get fired up to work today?"

"You'll find a way," Duke remarked. "Just dig down into that squirrel brain of yours."

Rafiq sauntered over and sat beside them. The drone traffic had increased as rush-hour hit its peak for the morning. Thousands of Crystalleans needing their breakfasts, new clothes, medicine, and contracts delivered to their towers. Rafiq sat beside them and began prattling on about a date he had last night. Cole and Duke looked at each other. That beautiful silence was gone. Duke raised a hand just above his lap.

"When was the last time you were over there?" Duke asked Rafiq.

"This off record? We off the clock?" Rafiq asked, his eyes shifting to Cole and Duke. They both nodded.

Rafiq licked his lips. "Last weekend, got to sneak into one of their underground clubs, the women are perfect—"

Duke raised his hand again and Rafiq stopped talking. "How do you get in?"

"I have my ways…why?"

Duke looked over at Cole and gave an upward nod. Cole shifted his stance and told them both everything.

Rafiq let out a whistle. "Sounds like she's in deep. How she going to turn off the tag?"

"I'll have to figure that out, but can you get me over there?" Cole said.

"When?" Rafiq asked.

"Tonight," Cole answered.

Duke and Rafiq exchanged glances. Duke went to speak, but noticed the electro-bus had arrived with the rest of the crew. "We'll discuss this later. Now get to work."

FIVE

By midday the mud had hardened to packed dirt and a steady breeze kept the workers cool. Cole setup the blueprints for the new pipe on a large board of plywood. He showed where the pipe ruptured the day before and where the new materials would need to be installed. The workers had been extra fast that day, embarrassed about yesterday's snafu. They didn't like disappointing Duke. They could care less about what Cole thought.

Duke summoned Rafiq and Cole to his office trailer over the PA system. They both hustled over to the white trailer with nicotine-stained blinds. Inside a small fan oscillated back and forth. Duke's graying chest hair followed the direction of the wind. The ember of the cigar glowed bright as Duke took a long drag from it. A thick blanket of smoke lingered overhead.

"Rafiq, you take the Echo-Route into Crystalline, right?" Duke asked.

Rafiq's eyes widened. "How do you know that?"

Duke grinned. "So that's a yes." He looked from above his small reading glasses. "Is that the only route?"

Rafiq, now embittered, mumbled "Yes."

"And clothing, what do you do about that? Surely if anyone saw the crap you wear, you'd be arrested on the spot."

"My contact has a trunk of outfits before the tunnel," Rafiq said, looking Cole up and down. "I'm sure Harvard-boy can fit into it, but you're going to need something special."

"Don't worry about me."

Cole noticed the sun falling toward the horizon and began to grow anxious. He thought of Ainsley having to spend another night in danger. Pushing the thought from his mind, he spoke. "What is the city like? How are you not detected when you go in?"

"I blend into the crowds. If I'm not hitting the clubs, I go to the bazaar. I score what I want and bounce. Both spots are always packed, so it's easier to hide. I've never walked around the city, but if you're dressed right and don't get stopped by the guards, you'll be fine."

Cole sighed. There were still too many variables unaccounted for.

Duke consulted the map Cole had given him. "You said your sister lives in Pylône Sept. That's several blocks from Echo-route's exit. We can't use any monorails or taxis, as that requires a Crystallean RFID tag. I'm guesstimating a twenty minute walk."

"That's not too bad…right?" Cole said.

"The scanners will be out," Rafiq added.

"Scanners?" Cole asked.

Duke and Rafiq looked at Cole, taking pity on the rookie. Rafiq motioned to Duke to explain. Duke took off his glasses and looked up at Cole. "The guards inside Crystalline are the twenty-first century Gestapo. They demand order and will haul your ass out if you're a threat. That is why the social graph is so important to them. Once your number dips below threshold, you're finished. They come looking for you. Some people try and flee, but the scanner drones usually get them. They're spherical and cast red beams down on the citizens." Duke paused and looked through the blinds at Crystalline. "If you're caught in their crosshairs, you're finished."

Cole didn't say anything at first. He processed his fear and suppressed it. "Where do violators go?" Cole asked.

"I'm not sure. Somewhere unpleasant. We had one worker years ago get caught, haven't seen him since," Duke answered.

"How do you know all this?"

"When they were building the city, I had a few contracts with Janus, but eventually we weren't *good enough* for them because I don't have any social network scores."

They sat in silence for a long time. In the distance, machinery cawed and buzzed. Most of the workers were finishing up for the day. Through the blinds, the first shimmers of light appeared from the purple cityscape. Cole felt like he was standing before a great beast. Frightened and outmatched. The thought of Ainsley kept him from acting succumbing to his doubts. Closing his eyes, Cole thought of what would need to happen. *Get in, get out. Before sunrise.* If Rafiq could party inside the city, surely they could push through undetected.

"If we're going to do this," Duke said, "we'll need to get to the tunnels soon."

Rafiq, who had been leaning lazily against the wall, stood up straight and stretched. Duke nodded and looked at Cole. "We doing this, kid?"

Cole looked out at Crystalline. The drone traffic made blurs of light in between the high towers, a gentle fog approaching from the east. He looked out for red beams from the scanners. Cole turned to his colleagues and nodded. The three left the office trailer and headed to meet the woman who made entry to the city possible. Her name was Zelda.

SIX

The trio rode the electro-bus to the edge of town, closer to the Crystalline walls. As the motor's monotonous hum slowed, Rafiq stood up. "We're here," he said. Duke stared at the empty driver's seat and grunted. They climbed off the bus and crossed the damp street to a two story building that looked like an old mechanic's garage. The sign above the door read: *Tollbooth Café*. Duke held the door open for Cole and Rafiq.

A skinny woman with jet-black hair and pointy elbows watched the new patrons enter and rolled her eyes when she saw Rafiq. A vinyl record player spun Herbie Hancock's "Chameleon." and high beat jazz filled the café. The smell of freshly baked croissants and roasted coffee reminded Cole how hungry he was.

"What do you want, Rafiq? You come here too much," the woman behind the counter said.

"I'm trying to be your number one customer, Zelda."

Zelda ignored him and nodded her head at Duke and Cole. "What can I get ya?"

They ordered coffees and a mix of pastries. Zelda got to work and kept an eye on the last customer who was finishing up his evening Danish and newspaper. Once he left, Duke took a seat and started reading the left-behind newspaper. He sensed this would take awhile, and got comfortable. Zelda came out from behind the counter and locked the front door of the café. Turning, she glared at Rafiq. "You can't come here twice in one week. People will get suspicious."

Rafiq looked puzzled and insulted. "I buy coffee, don't I?"

"You also take a cross-town bus for a measly cup of coffee; it's an anomaly in patterns."

Cole perked up hearing this. Drinking his warm coffee that tasted like currant and cocoa, he moved passed Zelda and looked behind the counter. Just as he expected, he saw the blue and green glow from underneath the register.

An Orion-Tau MK 24, one of the first personal-supercomputers. It had been years since he saw one. The last time he used one was at MIT.

"Hey!" Zelda shouted.

Cole leaned back fast, spilling coffee on his hand. He licked it off his knuckles and set the saucer down. "Sorry. I just haven't seen a system like that in a long time."

"And what would you know about it? If you're friends with Rafiq you probably want to use it for some crypto-mine hacking. I run a clean shop, okay?"

"Relax, Zelda," Rafiq said. "Cole's like you, all smart and stuff. He went to Harvard."

"MIT," Cole corrected him.

Zelda looked Cole up and down. "Then what are you doing hanging out with these two gorillas?"

"I work with them. It's honest work. Can you help us or not?"

Zelda nodded and went back behind the counter. "You need to go behind the wall, pay the toll and go." She motioned to a stack of linen coffee bean bags. Cole imagined it was some sort of false wall like he'd seen inside Monticello.

"Thanks Zelda," Rafiq said, pulling out his wallet.

"Hang on." Cole pushed Rafiq away. "How much to use your system?"

Zelda smirked. "Not for sale buddy, these things can be tracked the second you do anything illegal. The Department of Cyber Protection would swarm here in minutes."

Cole laughed. "You're afraid of *them*? C'mon, you're telling me you have a rig like that and don't know how to cover your tracks?" Cole continued to laugh. He knew Zelda was a coder at heart. All coders hate to have their ability laughed at.

Zelda stood there brooding. "Of course I can," she blurted out, "How do you think I keep a café like this running? I run several businesses from that thing. And you cannot use it."

Rafiq stood by, closely observing the scuffle. He loved watching arguments. Cole noticed this and handed Rafiq a muffin. "Go stand in the corner." Cole pushed him away. Rafiq complied.

"Look, I get it. If I had a rig like that, I'd be in a secure building plugged in all day. But I'm dealing with a family crisis." Cole took the Polaroid from his pocket and slid it across the counter. "This is my sister Ainsley. She's stuck over there and I need to get her out of Crystalline. I've learned today about the tagging every Crystallean has."

"You just learned about that?" Zelda said.

Cole nodded. "Have you ever turned one off? I need to know more about them. I'll pay you whatever you want."

Zelda drummed her nails in a rhythm on the black granite countertop. She glanced at the photo again. "Who did this to her?"

"Her husband. He's a high-ranking official in the Crystalline government."

"Prick." Zelda rubbed her arms, remembering old wounds of her own. "How long has this been going on?"

"I don't know, but she says she only has thirty-six hours."

Zelda's eyes widened. "Oh fuck, she's on the clock?"

"I guess."

"Oh jeez, she did something bad. She said that? Thirty-six hours, you're sure?" Zelda asked. Cole nodded. Zelda stood back. "Rafiq, Gigantor, you two watch the door. Cole, come to my office. There's something I need to show you."

SEVEN

Zelda led Cole upstairs to a dusty office. The place was surrounded by linen coffee sacks and piles of old magazines. The windows had been spray-painted white, though a small hole was scratched out as a makeshift peephole. On a threadbare couch a calico cat lay curled up in a purple sweater. She opened her eyes at Cole and Zelda and then returned to sleep, uninterested.

The thin barista sat down at her pine desk and tapped three keys on her computer. Several computer screens, mounted on gimbals, slivered up from behind the desk and powered on, displaying a landscape view of Monument Valley. A command prompt filled part of the screen and Zelda began to type. A moment later dozens of security camera videos showed the outside area of a place he'd never seen before. A city, completely spotless, no gum on the streets, no urine leaking from the corners of buildings. The people looked attractive and well groomed. It was like a city occupied by runway models.

"Crystalline?" Cole asked.

Zelda nodded, still typing. More security camera feeds flashed on screen. Subway stations, farmer's markets, soccer stadiums, the feeds flew by until it stopped on a group of uniformed men. A dry tingle of horror struck Cole. These men were clad in black pants, white button-downs with black ties, a gold badge, and officer hats that looked to be taken from 1940s Russia. They were marching almost robotically, passing Crystalleans averted their eyes and moved on, like they were avoiding a pack of wolves. The men wore strange headsets across their eyes that emitted a red beam.

"The Crystalline Guard," Zelda said. "They're real pieces of work."

"What's up with those headsets?" Cole asked.

"They're scanners that feed directly to the Praetorians, the elite guards for government officials."

"But it looks like some of the regular people have them on too?"

She glanced at the screen Cole was looking at. "Same tech. It's a way for people to continue work as they commute home. Everyone has a headset.

Anyway, let me find it…" Zelda leaned in closer to the screen, still cycling through the various feeds. "Ahh ha, here we are." A feed showed a gothic stone building with the stark resemblance of an Austrian cathedral. Beyond the foreground tall spires rose above the city in front of a starry night. "Pylône Sept."

"That's where Ainsley— wait, how do you know where she lives?"

Zelda smirked. "My system downstairs scanned your face and showed me your family history. I do this to all my customers." She tapped just below her eye, indicating the AR-contact lenses. "Your sis is married to a head honcho."

"I'm sure you know more than me. How did you get access to this?"

"Because I'm the most brilliant programmer this side of the Mississippi. Anyway, if your sister needs extraction, she'll have to turn off the RFID device; good news is I've made something that can do this." Zelda opened a drawer and took out an old radio that had a small green screen and rubber buttons on it. "Easy to use: turn it on, follow the instructions." Zelda tossed it to Cole.

Cole was silent, his eyebrows raised. "How'd you…why'd you?"

Zelda unrolled her sleeve, showing a scar just below her left wrist, "When I was young and stupid, I fell in love with a Crystallean. Washboard abs, no debt, access to anything, and the fame, who can resist?"

"Why'd you leave?"

Zelda shrugged. "Free speech, the innate luxury all Americans are born with, is just as strong a gift as us having opposable thumbs. We only learn the true power of our gifts after they're taken away. Crystalline has their own version of free speech. They silence anyone who doesn't think *their* way. Crystallean babies are born with social media accounts reserved for them. Apparently they're now being optimized for top health and aesthetics when in the womb, but that's just a rumor. Either way, it's total madness."

Cole nodded. He'd heard about the lengths these people would take in order to raise their social rankings. He noticed it when his sister no longer wanted to debate something, whether it was politics or movies. She simply didn't want to hear opposing arguments. "So…you just sit here and stalk them? What's your end goal here?"

Zelda rubbed the scar on her arm. "To free those people. They're trapped and they don't know it. I collect as much data as I can to help people like you."

"I'm just here to help my sister, that's all. I'm not interested in trying to overthrow some city of privilege."

"Even after they've hurt her?"

"It's a rescue. Not an attack."

Zelda stood and walked over to Cole, her eyes misty. "Once you see the madness of that city, you'll change your mind."

Cole understood her pain, but he felt he was wasting time. "Are you going to help me or not?"

Zelda sighed and sat back down in front of the screens. She pulled up a live map of the city. "You'll be entering through the purple line subway tunnels. Rafiq knows where to go. I've seen a spike in scanner activity near the tunnels lately, so be cautious."

"What about clothes?"

She pointed at a Japanese blind. In front of it sat a large trunk. "Start going through that. I'm sure there's something in your size." Zelda faced the computer. "What the hell?" On screen a convoy of white electric-SUVs pulled up in front of Pylône Sept. A dozen guards hustled out and marched into the building.

"Can you see what is going on inside?"

"No, but I can try; it'll take time to sift around the security system of an apartment buildings like hers. This isn't good, Cole. You need to get there now."

EIGHT

Cole and Zelda hurried down the stairs, their footsteps sounding like muffled drumbeats. Rafiq and Duke looked up from their coffees, concerned.

"The Crystalline Guard just swarmed Ainsley's building. They're coming for her. They must be." Cole ran his hands through his hair, holding on to the back of it tightly. "We need to get to her now."

Zelda nodded. "Cole's right. The amount of men that arrived is troubling."

"We can't fight them all off," Rafiq stated. "It's just three of us."

Duke sat back with his arms folded, nodding.

"Oh, so you're backing out?" Cole said, his voice a little higher than normal.

Duke ignored Cole and looked at Zelda. "What's your experience been with these guards?"

Zelda shrugged. "Crystalline Guards are all equipped with headsets that feed into the Praetorian headquarters. You *don't* want those guys showing up. So I wouldn't recommend messing with them if you don't have to."

Rafiq said, "Zelda can you hook us up with some weapons? Guns, tasers—"

"The fuck do I look like?" Zelda scoffed. "I deal with ones and zeros."

Duke reached to the small of his back and pulled out a chrome .357 snub nose revolver. "I have this, but eight rounds won't cut it."

Cole and Rafiq looked surprised at Duke.

"What? I live in a bad neighborhood."

"Great, we're going into the world's most advanced future city with a hand cannon from last century," Rafiq muttered.

"Either way, going up against any of the guards in Crystalline is bound to get you all killed. They're all connected to each other. Like a terrible virus capable of attacking multiple hosts at once," Zelda said.

Cole kicked a stool out from under a table with his foot and sat, sighing. He saw the reflection of the Crystalline skyline in the oblong mirror that hung above the espresso machine. The pink neon glow was magnified by tonight's fog. Zipper lines of green and orange drone traffic dotted through the lower blankets of fog. He thought of Ainsley. Was she looking out her window at the gray and yellow skyline of Old City, wondering if she'd ever be free? He put his hands in his jacket pockets and felt the vial the man at the Woo Fong Apothecary gave him. Cole took it out and examined it.

"What do you make of this?" Cole asked, handing it over to Zelda.

Zelda squinted at the finger floating in gel. A look of disgust and fascination grew across her face.

"Christ Cole, you sick bastard," Rafiq said, thoroughly repulsed.

Zelda smirked. "Clever. You get this at the apothecary in Chinatown?"

Cole nodded. "What's the deal with that place?"

"It's one of the oldest smuggling houses in the lower forty-eight. Mr. Fong may have given you a ticket into Pylône Sept." Zelda put a black painted nail against a tiny label on the cap of the vial. Cole leaned in and saw it read: *J. Billows 13 - Pylône Sept.*

"Sonofabitch, how'd I miss that?" Cole said, sitting back.

Zelda handed the vial back to Cole and flicked her head up. "How much that run you?"

Cole looked confused. "Nothing…he just gave it to me."

Zelda gave a sarcastic chuckle. "Wow kid, you just keep getting more interesting. Mr. Fong doesn't do anything for free. He'll probably want something from you sooner or later."

"Lucky me." Cole sighed.

"This is good luck, Cole. With this finger you can scan right into the building and walk straight past the guards. Just don't let them directly see you."

Cole looked at Rafiq and Duke. They gave a nod. "Tick tock," Duke said.

They adjourned from the café and went back upstairs to find Crystallean clothes in their sizes. Duke was the most difficult one to find an outfit for. It was like trying to outfit Thor in the kid's department at the mall. He gave up and kept the clothes he was wearing, but grabbed a black trench coat that fit snugly around his body. He flicked the collar up and winked at Rafiq, who rolled his eyes in return.

"You look like a flasher," Rafiq commented.

"Can it," Zelda said. "Give me your pay-card. I'll need to reload it so you have some walking around money. I'll add it to your tab."

"Thanks," Rafiq said, a bit perturbed on how many commas were on that tab by now.

Cole stepped out from the Japanese blind. He wore slacks that were synthetic material but had a crease starting at the knee. His shirt was white, and the silver zipper started at the knob of his left shoulder and sliced across his chest down to his right hip. Over that was a dark purple rain jacket. Pulling on a pair of boots, he felt small motors humming beneath the arch of his foot. He looked up at Zelda, confused.

She was eating a croissant for dinner. "Remember that old movie with the DeLorean?"

"No way…these have auto-laces?"

Zelda smiled. Cole admired her for a moment. She did have a beautiful smile; the kind that floods a face like ink spilling on white tablecloth. "Something like that." She walked back to her computer. The screen airing Pylône Sept still showed a crew of guards in their white electric-SUVs. The guards were milling about the area, seemingly bored. One guard was doing pushups, which seemed odd to Zelda. *But then again, this whole city is odd,* she thought quietly to herself. She whispered at the screen, "What are you preparing for?"

* * *

The crew was suited up in Crystallean garb. Cole was fiddling with the device that would deactivate the RFID tracker. Zelda explained that it needed to be held above the tracker, most likely on her arm, and to let it scan into the system. "It won't deactivate it entirely. It scrambles the internal workings, but eventually it'll reboot itself and start functioning again. You'll want to remove it if possible." Cole listened, looking pale. "Your med-kit has a small scalpel and bandages which should do the trick." Zelda realized she was being too blunt, a problem she'd always dealt with. She never understood why fluff needed to be added to conversations. Just say what you need to say. She rested her hand on Cole's shoulder and looked into his sea green eyes. "You're going to do fine, Cole."

Cole nodded.

Zelda placed the device in his hands. "Get in. Keep your head down. Use Mr. Billow's finger to gain entry to the apartment—"

"Grab Ainsley, deactivate the RFID tracker, and get the hell out."

"See, you got this Cole. I've sent plenty of people over there to accomplish far stupider feats, they've all made it back."

"Glad I'm in fine company." Cole muttered.

Zelda shook her head and laughed. "C'mon, time to get going."

Cole took two deep breaths to get himself ready, like he was about to jump into a freezing lake. He stood, pulling on a black backpack which felt heavy, and looked at Zelda.

She sat with her arms folded. "I slid a bulletproof plate in there, just in case."

Cole didn't respond. He walked downstairs with Rafiq and Duke. Zelda scurried ahead of them and unlocked her basement door with an iris scanner. "Safe travels," was the last thing he heard as the door slid shut and locked. Dirty yellow lights illuminated the staircase. The air smelled damp, like old coffee left out in a winter shed. The basement was long and narrow. The walls were lined with gray steel shelves, holding forgotten coffee roasting equipment. Another shelving unit housed dozens of technical textbooks. Biochemistry, computer engineering, gene-therapy, and a copy of Asimov's *Foundation Trilogy*.

"This way," Rafiq said, as he turned down a sloped corridor that Cole could barely see in the dim yellow light. The walls and ceiling were red brick. Lightbulbs housed in protective metal lined the way. Duke's shoulders squeezed through the hall. He stayed behind Cole and moved on carefully. They walked for a long time. Cole was certain they'd surpassed the floor plan of the Tollbooth Café. Soon Cole saw the end of the hallway: a plain metal door. Rafiq held his hand out, readying to open it without breaking stride when he disappeared before Cole's eyes. Cole blinked and looked ahead, only seeing the metal door. Rafiq had vanished. Cole tried the knob but it was locked.

"What the...?" Cole turned around to face Duke and noticed a sliver of a void in the brick wall on his left. Cole slowly stepped forward. Sweat beaded along his forehead. Then a hand emerged out from the void. Cole jumped back. The hand came closer and soon the grinning face of Rafiq was revealed.

"Gotcha bitch," Rafiq said.

"What the hell is this?"

Rafiq took out a flashlight and pointed it down a pitch black pathway with a dirt ground. "Zelda built this narrow off-chute as a redirect. Clever right?"

"Let's keep moving," Duke grunted.

They made their way down the off-chute, the three pairs of feet crunching and scraping along the dirt path. Soon it ended at a metal door that still held some shine despite being caked in red dust. Rafiq tapped a numeric keypad; he punched in the code and the door lazily gasped. Cole was expecting a futuristic door that slid open, like on the Starship Enterprise. Instead the door listed pathetically on squeaky hinges, like a palm leaf in the wind. Rafiq opened the door with his foot and shone the flashlight on both sides before stepping in further.

They entered a wide tunnel which was lit by red utility lights. The tunnel ran perpendicular to the entryway. Duke shut the door behind him. The tunnel had rails running along the ground. "We're in the subways? All that to get into the subway tunnels?"

Rafiq shook his head. "Hyperloop service tunnels. These were the original ones they built for testing purposes. They're mostly out of commission."

"Mostly?" Cole asked.

"Yeah…don't worry, there are apparently hundreds of levels of tunnels." Rafiq was shining the light against the far wall, searching for something. Cole pointed his flashlight against the wall and noticed a chalked arrow pointing right. Rafiq saw it too and followed its direction. They walked on, their light beams bouncing in the darkness through the red tunnel, as if descending into hell. Everyone was mostly silent except for the occasional cough. It was musty down there and had that drywall smell only found at construction sites. It made them all think about work. They thought of telling stories, but held off. Better to remain quiet in case a tunnel train traveling at the speed of a bullet sneaks up on them. Cole wondered if you'd feel any pain being hit by one. *Probably not.* He thought it would be one big *splat.*

None of them feared the darkness of the tunnel. Working in construction makes you shelve any types of worry about industrial spaces. They all thought, but would never admit, that this was better than being out in the woods where there are bears, forest fires and lunatics. The worst they'd see was a rat.

An hour had passed and it started to feel that they were stuck inside some continuous loop. Cole couldn't remember when the tunnel started banking slightly right, but it seemed it hadn't stopped. Twice Cole thought about raising this to Rafiq, but didn't want to start an argument.

Far in the distance Cole spotted a white beam of light. It expanded like an optical illusion has he approached. Rafiq held up a closed fist. "Shut the lights off boys, we're getting close." What they heard next was something no one expected: laughter.

* * *

Duke squinted through the darkness toward the laughter, which was answered with an even more disturbing cackle. Rafiq, Duke and Cole crept forward toward the light. The call-and-repeat laughter-cackle response echoed throughout the dark tunnel. A chill ran down Cole's spine. He watched Duke reach into the small of his back and pull out the revolver. *If he fires in the tunnel, half the city will hear it,* Cole thought.

Then they saw it. A guard floating above them atop the white light. It looked as if he and his rifle were levitating by some force they'd never understand. The guard laughed again, bending over, a deep guttural laugh. His long rifle lay perpendicular to his torso, held on by a strap. Rafiq, who was closest to the light, realized they were beneath an old subway platform. He whispered the discovery to Cole and Duke, who both nodded and sighed a breath of relief.

Rafiq lurked below the platform, right beneath the guard. Duke came close and Rafiq whispered something in his ear. Cole couldn't hear what he said. Duke cupped his hands and made a hissing sound. The laughter stopped. Footsteps echoed in the quiet tunnel. The guard stood at the edge and shone a searchlight before him. Moments later a second guard approached the platform with his rifle ready. The guards' ankles were now just above Rafiq and Duke. The cut of light made the two practically invisible. Cole, unsure of what was about to happen, hid further under the platform, out of the way of the searchlights.

At once Rafiq and Duke grabbed the ankles of the guards and heaved them off the platform, their heads striking the tiled ground and sliding them down onto the rails. Rafiq lay on top of both men's chests while Duke went over to deliver cross punches to their skulls each. Moments later the only sound was the panting of Rafiq and Duke. The two guards were unconscious.

"You think that's all of them?" Cole asked, worried.

"Let's hope. Grab the flex cuffs from their belts," Rafiq said.

Duke set the flashlight against the far wall, providing a wash of fading white light. They now could fully see the guards. Their uniforms made them look more like traffic cops: black slacks, white shirts with gold badges pinned to their hearts and black ties. Around both their necks were the headsets Cole saw the guards wearing from Zelda's computer. The headsets seemed to be turned off. Cole figured they must be overkill for patrolling a dead tunnel.

"Never underestimate man's laziness," Duke mused. "If what Zelda said is true and if these things were on, we'd be surrounded right now." Duke unhooked the headsets and tossed them down the tunnel.

Rafiq took utility tape from the belt of one of the guards and gagged them both. He looked up at Cole, who had a worried look. "They'll be fine," Rafiq said. They left the two guards bound and gagged beside the rails.

The three men climbed onto the platform and squinted through the overhead lights. Cole dusted himself off and looked around. There was a staircase nearby. They crept slowly up the stairs while trying to listen for any other movement or laughter. It was quieter than a morgue. Ascending the stairs Cole spoke softly. "Hey Rafiq, is this the way you normally go?"

"Nah man," Rafiq said keeping his eyes forward. "I never noticed the platform before. The lights must've always been out. I use a different exit shaft. But if this map is correct, it just put us closer to Pylône Sept."

At the top of the stairs was a glass turnstile. The entire area was dimly lit, running on auxiliary power. They moved through the turnstile door, which was propped open with an orange traffic cone. On the other side, the area widened and there were lockers and a punch clock scanner. This area was for workers doing shift changes. Beyond the lockers was a steel door which was also propped open with a cone. The team slowly scurried around the obstacle and pushed through. The air began to smell different, less damp, more fresh.

Past the door was another hallway which ended at the bottom of a spiral staircase. Cole looked through the slits in the black stairs and saw the tall neon spires of Crystalline and beyond that a glimmer of the Milky Way. He felt like he was on a ship somewhere in space beyond the Kuiper Belt. Feeling closer to Ainsley made him grin.

They ascended the spiraling stairs and emerged in an alleyway between two high-rise buildings. No guards in sight. They hurried out of the alley and onto the sidewalk. Duke and Cole couldn't help but look up again at the magnificent purple-pink hue the skyscrapers gave off in the pre-dawn light. It was like swimming in an O'Keeffe watercolor.

Rafiq rubbed his hands together, smiling. "Welcome to Crystalline, gents."

NINE

The sun peaked over the cornfields at the edge of the earth, casting golden light against the spires of Crystalline. A brief shower came and went before dawn and the air smelled sweet. Lavender clouds ran across the fields in front of an apricot sky. With each passing minute the drones emerged from their charging centers in the Utility District and formed a holding pattern around the city. They were hovering twenty stories above the streets, like a swarm of locusts, ready to get to work. When the atomic clock struck 0600HRS they buzzed forward in predetermined paths. By 0605 some were already making contact with the sky-rise delivery ports, delivering fresh groceries from Farmer's District and the morning mail. Housekeeping drones swept and cleaned apartments.

Cole and Duke marveled at this sight. They'd watched the traffic patterns from a distance but being *under* the traffic was something different. They couldn't believe they occupied the same time period. The tech Cole read about in his science-fiction comics were now real. He wondered quietly who the urban planners of this city were and if they too read Clarke, Asimov and Robinson. Rafiq kept looking over his shoulder, hoping no guards were tailing them.

"Can we check the map?" Rafiq asked.

Cole nodded and they leaned against a corrugated wall of a containership that was retrofitted to house expensive athletic clothing. Duke peered through the window and spotted the price on a sports bra and his jaw dropped.

"Here, we're on Parker Way. This can take us to Mantis Drive, which'll put us on some sort of bike path toward Pylône Sept," Cole said.

"Morning!" said a jovial voice. It made the three jump. There they saw a man on an electric bicycle. The three gave a tired nod and smile. The man zipped by, a series of other cyclists following suit. The buzzing sounds reverberated off the corrugated wall. The cyclists were a mix of men and women, all of them phenomenally fit. None had an ounce of unnecessary flab budging from the common areas. They moved by delivering greetings as they were in a campy cereal commercial from the 1990s.

"Morning guys."

"Good morning!"

"Morning!"

"On your left, friend."

Cole and Duke nodded, smiling and waving like they were at a parade they didn't want to participate in. Rafiq kept a watch out for the guards. He was getting nervous.

The peloton passed and continued down the road like a herd of gliding antelopes. "Seems to be friendly enough over here," Duke commented.

Rafiq shook his head. "They *have* to do that. Greeting strangers is an easy point-gainer for them."

Duke looked confused. "Even *that* will get ranked?"

Rafiq nodded.

Duke shook his head, chuckling. "Of course."

They walked on, favoring pedestrian paths that avoided the roads. Even though it was the early morning, the city was bustling with people. Soon they came upon a farmer's market. Autonomous trucks were caked in red dust from hauling fresh vegetables from the fields of Farmer's District. A cold morning dew peppered the windshields. Men in overalls and women in bandanas unloaded the produce onto a conveyor belt which rolled everything through a scanner. Cole looked into the eyes of the farmer on the other end of the conveyor belt. She looked upset as she tossed fine looking apples and squashes into a trash receptacle.

Rafiq put his knuckle into Cole's back to keep him from slowing down. "They only allow *perfect* food to be sold to Crystalleans. Photogenic food is as important as the nutrition it provides."

Another stall had a medley of vegetables and fruits, all various shades of red, yellow and purple. A collection of glass vials held powders and other elixirs. An impossibly beautiful blonde woman mixed the ingredients into a massive blender to make juices and smoothies. Rafiq looked for a free sample, but none were around.

"Eyes up," Duke muttered.

Cole and Rafiq looked ahead and saw the Crystalline Guard marching straight toward them. They moved in tandem, an elegant march made their boots sound like a continuous drumbeat. These guards were dressed in similar uniform to the two guards they met earlier, but these men were all in a monochrome shade of steel. The only color were the green scopes of their rifles and the orange headsets. Cole edged back and bumped into Rafiq, who nudged him to keep moving forward, toward the approaching guards.

"If they spotted us, we'd know it by now. Move on and keep your eyes away from them," Rafiq said.

Cole, thinking quickly, didn't want to take any chance and turned back, fighting Rafiq's hand. Cole hurried over to the juicer stall and spoke to the blonde woman. He ordered three smoothies as the march of the boots grew closer. Cole glanced over his shoulder and saw they were no more than twenty yards away. Duke was reaching for his pistol.

"Hey guys!" Cole shouted. "Breakfast is on me."

Duke pulled his hand away and walked toward Cole. Rafiq rolled his eyes and followed.

They all leaned against the bar and watched the pretty blonde woman grind up carrots and pears. She smiled at them and added the powders and strange brown liquids that moved like cold maple syrup. The blender drowned out the sound of the boots. When she finished, they turned and watched the guards walk on.

"There y'all go gentlemen, enjoy!" she said in an accent Cole thought to be from Louisiana. She loaded up other canisters of smoothies into a drone that had landed nearby.

Duke took a sip and pulled back repulsed. "What is this? Mulch and mud?"

"No idea," Cole said, sipping his and wincing. "C'mon let's keep moving."

They later passed a gym that had large glass windows facing the street. Everyone inside was working on chrome and wire machines. It looked like a collection of Bernini statues trying to recreate the antique film *Pumping Iron*.

Soon they walked through what Cole figured should be named *Vanity Row* as it was littered with tanning salons, collagen injection facilities, detox centers, cryotherapy pods and, of course, life coaching offices. Cole came to the end of the row and spotted a sign for Mantis Way. They turned left and after several blocks they came upon Pylône Sept. Something was different from when he last saw it on the video feed at Zelda's. All of the Crystalline Guard's white electric-SUVs had left.

A pit grew in Cole's stomach and he felt his knees buckle. They had taken Ainsley. They were too late. She was gone.

TEN

"When did they leave?" Cole asked into the phone.

"Unclear. Before dawn they just packed up and left. I tried calling but you were underground," Zelda said.

Cole pulled the phone away from his ear and cursed.

"Cole?"

"Yes," he said despondently. "I'm here."

"They didn't have Ainsley. I've reviewed the security footage. I'm certain."

A tinge of hope, like the first sip of tea on a cold night, warmed him. "She's still inside?"

"Most likely, but it looks like they kept some guards at the apartment," Zelda warned.

"Yeah, I saw one mulling around outside," Cole said. He peeked from the alleyway he was hiding in while Rafiq and Duke circled the apartment looking for a secondary entrance.

"I have to go. I need to open the café. Text me if you need anything else," Zelda said.

"Okay, will do…thanks Zelda." Cole hung up.

Rafiq and Duke rounded the corner into the alleyway. Both of them shook their heads. Cole stamped the ground and swore again. He took the vial out of his pocket and examined the finger floating inside. It was their only way in. Cole unscrewed the black cap and a pungent smell leaked out, similar to the scent of a titan arum flower. Dumping the liquid in a storm drain, Cole pulled the finger out of the vial with a handkerchief and patted it dry. The finger was olive colored and the nail a blackish purple. Rafiq watched him uneasily. Duke kept a lookout.

Cole held the severed finger between his thumb and index finger and pulled his sleeve to cover the strange sight. The finger felt cold and mushy, like raw chicken. He nodded to himself, saying he could do this. Cole thought of Ainsley and that pushed the fear down but didn't kill it. Nothing ever truly killed fear. It lingered with a protracted half-life.

"Alright," Cole said as he breathed heavily. "You guys stay behind me. Stay close." Before Duke and Rafiq could say anything, Cole was already walking fast toward Pylône Sept.

From a distance Pylône Sept looked like it was built in eighteenth-century France. The tall neo-gothic spires, some with Christian adornments, were still black against the morning light. A series of archways were glowing like great hearths. Cole could see the detail of the marble frieze wrapping above the archways. It looked to be a utopian scene, farmers and doctors and mothers helping each other. Duke noticed the frieze too and something uneasy grew inside him; he swallowed the concern, a talent only developed from age.

The classical elements of the building's design faded when they approached the foyer. The interior looked sleek and modern. Elephant ear plants lined the walkway toward a double glass door. Beside it was the finger scanner and video screen, both of them off. Through the glass he noticed a lobby with Barcelona chairs, sharp lighting features jutting from the ceiling like stalagmites, and a narrow fireplace made from black and white marble. The fire feathered to and fro in a calculated dance as all gas fires do. A front desk, which looked more like a polished moon rock, stood unoccupied.

Cole held Mr. Billow's finger against the scanner. The video screen came to life showing it scanning the ridges and valleys of the severed digit. A moment passed, then another, and soon it tallied up to a minute. The screen flashed red and a disapproving buzz sounded twice. *"Identity Confirmation Error, please use facial identification."*

Before Cole knew what was happening a white light flashed on from above the screen. Cole turned away shielding himself from the spotlight.

"No, no, no," Cole said, moving away.

They all turned and hurried out of the foyer, passing the beautifully lined plants and under the archways again back out onto the street. Duke thought he heard the marching sound of boots and checked over his shoulder. There he saw four Crystalline Guards exiting through the front door.

"Pick up the pace, fellas," Duke said.

Rafiq and Cole gave a worried look over their shoulders and they went from a speed walk to a trot and then to a run. Moments later they were back in the alleyway where Cole had been speaking to Zelda. The guards didn't pursue. It looked to them like they were early morning commuters heading out to get coffee.

"Goddammit," Cole said, stuffing the finger back in the vial. "It must've decayed too much. I don't want to risk it again."

Rafiq and Duke looked at Cole, wondering what to do next. Cole propped his back against the wall and slid down to sit on his heels. He dipped his head and thought again of Ainsley. She needed him. He couldn't leave his sister, not when he'd come this far. Cole looked up at the first streaks of white clouds in the morning sky. It was shaping up to be a beautiful day. A couple of drones buzzed along at twenty stories up. Beyond that he noticed a jetliner making fresh trails of white in its atmospheric wake.

Something struck Cole. He stood up and tried to single out a drone from the flurry of traffic. It was like trying to lock on one bee in a swarm. Soon he succeeded by watching one slow and veer off course towards an apartment building adjacent to Pylône Sept. Its flaps flared and reflected the sun's light as it came feet from the building. Then it scurried into a chute and disappeared like a bee entering a honeycomb. Cole stared at the building for a long time and noticed a series of chutes every couple of floors. He figured they were ventilation ducts but now realized they were delivery ports. Cole grinned and pulled out his phone.

A couple miles away Zelda was carefully making a latte design in a wide coffee mug. It was quite beautiful in fact, two bears sitting beside a honeypot, an art Zelda taught herself because she noticed that young twenty-somethings were likely to pay more for some milk and coffee if it had a children's drawing on the top. *What imbeciles*, she'd thought to herself, but then shrugged as she calculated the increased revenues. Beside the steaming silver mug of milk was her phone which began to vibrate. A new encrypted message alert flashed within her contact lens.

The message read: "Can a person fit in drone-mailer? ;-)"

✳ ✳ ✳

Cole, I thought you were the brains here. Even *I* know this is a dumb idea," Rafiq said.

"They transport pets across town in these things. You can breathe in the pods," Cole said confidently.

"Yeah, cause if fucking Fido dies they'll just clone another," Rafiq said.

"Oh I'm sorry," Cole said annoyed, "did you have any other plans on getting into the apartment? Let's hear them, Rafiq. Right now. Go on, tell me."

Rafiq said nothing. He crossed his arms and walked away from Cole. Duke stepped as if they were in a tag-team wrestling match in logic and sensibility.

Duke looked at Cole and then at the buzzing of the drone traffic above. He put a hand on Cole's shoulder and exhaled. Cole could smell his sour breath. "Look kid…if you're going to do this…don't wiggle around too much on the inside," he said with a smirk.

"Duke!" Rafiq said.

"Thanks, Duke," Cole said, returning the smile.

"I think Rafiq should join you in another drone."

"What?" Rafiq said. "No way, nah-uh."

Cole's phone started buzzing. It was Zelda. "Hey, any progress?" Cole asked.

"Yes, but…"

"What?"

"Well if I'm going to do this, I'll need to double my rate. I can't take this level of risk without being compensated."

Cole didn't say anything for a moment.

"Cole?" Zelda said.

"Whatever it costs, I'll pay it."

"Okay then, sending the specs to you now."

Cole's screen projected a three-dimensional schematic of a Stribog Mailer Drone 39a constructed by the Janus Corporation. The design rotated before him. It looked like two silver coffins stacked on top of each other, with six arm propellers jutting from the center. Small fins and landing gear lay flush against the fuselage.

"How tall are you, Cole? And please don't give me a male answer."

Cole scoffed, but then subtracted the two inches he typically added.

"Alrighty and you probably weigh well under two-hundred pounds?"

"Correct, one-sixty most days."

Zelda said nothing. All he heard was breathing and the clicking of her keyboard. "You can fit. It'll be tight but I'm pretty confident you'll fit. Good thing it's not Duke we're sending over."

"Terrific, when will it—"

"60 seconds."

"What?"

"I've ordered a dog drone transporter to your location. You'll have three minutes to enter the pod, and it'll be a quick ride given the distance from you to Pylône Sept."

"Thank you Zelda."

"Good luck, Cole." The line went dead.

Twenty seconds later a hi-lo beep and chime alarm sounded. A search light shone directly above Cole. He noticed the center of the beam had a green laser projecting a crosshair sign on the ground. The outer rim of the beam flashed yellow print: LANDING ZONE, STAY BACK. Dust scattered from its center and spewed to the sides. Cole, Rafiq and Duke covered their eyes for a moment. Seconds later the drone landed with the pod on the ground. The door opened up and blue lights filled the interior.

A mechanical voice spoke from the drone: "*Place canine inside the pod please.*" A rectangular screen projected a two minute countdown in red numbering.

Duke stood with arms crossed and looked at Cole and gave him a single nod, as if saying "Godspeed Major Tom." Rafiq stood there in disbelief. Cole looked into the blue pod and swallowed his apprehension and crawled inside. The pod door sealed shut.

"*Thank you. Step back please.*" The drone ascended slowly from the alleyway again, kicking up the recently settled dust.

The blue lights remained on inside the pod and Cole could see through one of the vent holes. Crystalline looked like a complex neon circuit board with charges of light running across all its connections. Similar to what synapses firing against neurons must look like, Cole mused. He thought for a moment this wasn't so bad, until the drone merged onto one of the routing ways and bolted forward at seventy miles an hour. Cole slid and gripped the inside of the drone instinctively when he noticed he somehow wasn't sliding. It was like the inertia glued him to the pod floor. The circuit board city blurred and the spires of high-rises edged by like pine needles against a train window. The humming of the motors slowed to a monotonous tone as it cruised over toward Pylône Sept.

The drone decelerated further and Cole noticed he was climbing higher than the twenty story cruising altitude. He could see through the side of the pod and saw floor to ceiling windows on the apartment units, then black metal, and then a chute. The drone passed that and kept climbing. Cole pushed the thoughts out of his head about what would happen if it didn't stop climbing. He remembered having this problem with the drone he played with as a child. "Sometimes the signals get crossed and there's nothing you can do but watch it climb to space," his father, Rex, once said. *Nothing you can do*, Cole repeated to himself, as if that would calm him down. Not having agency in a situation was enough to drive Cole Wainwright insane. The drone kept climbing and soon he saw the high arches of a balcony, something Rapunzel could look out from.

The drone stopped its ascent.

Nothing you can do Cole, it's just something that happens. Cole winced his eyes shut, making his father's voice drown out. Then he felt the drone edge forward and pause. It edged forward some more and paused, making calculated adjustments with the steady winds and the occasional gusts. Through the side, Cole saw the drone was threading between an archway onto the balcony. After several minutes of fits and starts it descended to the ground and the pod doors opened up. The lights all flashed green. A hi-lo beep and chime rang as Cole climbed out of the pod and onto the balcony.

He watched the drone do its calculated wiggle dance like a honeybee as it exited. Once it was through it dropped down in a nosedive several dozen stories and was lost in the gushing river of drone traffic. Cole took in the view of Crystalline. It was an angle he never expected to see. The sun had burned off the morning haze and a warm breeze rushed up the spire and through Cole's hair. The sky now was flawless blue and the amber fields in Farmer's District danced above green corn stalks.

"Hello?" said a worried but familiar voice, channeling a flood of memories. Cole smiled and turned. Standing there in a yellow cashmere sweater and faded blue jeans was Ainsley Wainwright.

ELEVEN

"Cole!" Ainsley shouted as she ran to his embrace. The high winds blew her red hair across his face. It was damp and smelled of shampoo. Ainsley pulled back and looked at her brother. Her hazel eyes looked like bulbs from pooling tears. "Cole…" She hugged him once more. After a moment she looked up at the skyline concerned. "We should get inside, there's no telling who's watching."

They walked through the wide balcony doors, passing long linen curtains which danced carelessly like a horse's tail in the wind. Ainsley shut the doors and locked them. Inside the apartment felt cool but not cold. The air was refreshing and there were lingering scents of mint and cucumber. The hickory floors were partially covered by animal hides, trip-color cows, zebras, antelope. All the furniture had sharp edges and exaggerated frames with exceptionally comfortable looking upholstery.

Ainsley called out to the AI home controller: "Marla, morning light and coffee and water please." An almost-human computerized voice acknowledged her command and the Venetian blinds adjusted slightly like the flaps on an airplane wing, letting daylight beam through in organized rows against the fireplace, which managed to light up on its own. Above the flame was a Gerardo Dottori painting of what looked to be a train hurling from the edge of the earth at an unimaginable speed. Cole sat in an Eames Chair and admired a gold statuette on the coffee table made by Umberto Boccioni. Cole smiled. His sister had been into Italian modern art since she was little.

"Cole, thank you for getting here so soon. Jesus Christ, I don't know where to begin," Ainsley said, pushing her hair behind both ears.

"What's the deal with this countdown timer?"

Ainsley slammed her eyes shut and tears fell out. "Oh Cole…"

"Ains, we can get you out of here. I have this." He took out the device to deactivate the RFID tracker. "It can temporarily deactivate—"

"I've handled that already." Ainsley said, holding up her forearm; a grizzly incision ran down it. The color and visible traces of surgical sealant proved it was a recent procedure. "But it's a bit more complicated than that, Cole." Ainsley paused and looked up at the ceiling, then at her brother. "I was pregnant."

Cole looked at her, "Was?"

Ainsley started weeping again and collapsed her head into her hands. Cole was troubled by seeing his sister cry. It was something he'd never seen her do. She was always the alpha. His gaze drifted to the low movement in the corner of the room. It was the server-bot, a ground drone about the size of a case of beer. It hummed over to Ainsley on a set of six by six carbon-fiber wheels. On its top was a Yerba mate gourd, steam dancing from the metal end of the straw. Ainsley picked it up and sipped from the straw. The server-bot wheeled over to Cole and delivered a mug of black coffee with three sugar cubes next to it; he hoped it was coincidence that the AI knew the precise way he took his coffee. Cole took the mug and the server-bot wheeled away out of sight.

Ainsley drank from the gourd straw, took a few deep breaths and wiped her eyes with the ends of the sleeves of her sweatshirt. "What do you know about in utero gene therapy?"

"Um, it's a technology to treat birth defects, right? Or predict if the child may have certain diseases and disorders?"

Ainsley shook her head. "That's how it *began*. A genome editing technology made for *preventative* treatment like heart defects or whatever. But now it's being used for something entirely different." She pulled from the gourd and cleared her throat as if preparing for a lecture. "The scientists who run the program apply the therapy as earlier as possible, when the embryo hasn't grown beyond a single cell. This ensures that the genetic changes will successfully propagate to every other cell of the embryo as it grows, divides and develops. But the Crystallean doctors and scientists are the best in the world and they saw this tech as a way to truly propagate the vision of Crystalline."

Cole stared at his sister in silence. He could see the fear in her eyes, but the belief in her voice on that last sentence, about fulfilling the Crystalline vision, it made him shudder. She still believed in whatever insane vision these people had, despite her own pain.

"Well they saw this opportunity and ran with it. They stretched the possibilities of the human genome beyond what we could ever have imagined." Ainsley said. She gave a disappointed face when Cole didn't make the connection. "Cole, we found a way to edit the genome in utero, to the *exact* specs you would want your child to be."

Cole said nothing.

Ainsley continued to spell it out for her little brother. "If you want a kid that'll grow up cancer free, six foot five, a skeletal frame strong enough to pack muscle on like a sculptor makes a statue..." she trailed off. "Cole, the Crystalleans will be the first super-race. And I don't mean that in the sense of the *übermensch*. We have all creeds, class, color in Crystalline. This is about the betterment—no—the burgeoning of humanity."

"But..." Cole said, leading Ainsley back to a plane of reality he could understand.

She sighed, "Yeah...but I can't—" she began to weep again. "The gene therapy isn't working on me. My body rejects it somehow."

"Sis, how many times have you had it done?"

She set the gourd on the table beside a copy of a *The System of Objects* and cupped her hands together. "Three," she whispered.

"Three times already?"

"No...I've been pregnant three times," Ainsley said coldly.

"How have—" Cole stopped himself right there and knew the atrocious answer.

"Martin makes me stop them. It's a policy he wrote into the functioning Crystalline constitution. A woman who doesn't respond to in utero gene therapy must have the baby aborted before the first trimester."

Cole didn't know what to say, struck by the awfulness of it all. Anyone decreeing what another person can do with their body makes no logical or moral sense.

"And if you think there's some humane reason for that timing you're wrong. It's so that no one finds out you *were* pregnant. It's keeping up appearances. Keep that social score up, keep the facade running like a theatre screen that never turns off; always on and performing for the people to marvel at, comment, admire, like, yearn for...ahh!" Ainsley threw the gourd across the room and out of nowhere the server-bot zipped over at an impossible speed, its top opened up, and caught the gourd. A tiny squeegee emerged from an electric arm and mopped up the residual drips. Then it scurried away.

Ainsley sat there weeping. "Cole, I'm broken, I'm an awful mother, I..."

Cole got up and sat beside his sister and held her. "Sis, you're a good person. You are. You've just gotten too wrapped up in this lunacy. You're way over your head."

She pulled back. "Way over my head?"

Cole knew that look all too well, the look of a pissed off sister.

"I graduated top of my class, top of my law class and sold two companies before I was twenty-seven, I've…" Ainsley seemed to get exhausted of herself. Her thoughts running back to the problem at hand. Cole thought about what options there were and where the hell this prick Martin was. He wondered what Rafiq and Duke were doing. His fight or flight response was slowly rising, like a snow owl waking on a cold winter morning. He knew his time was running out and Ainsley needed to get beyond the city walls soon.

"Ains, we should go. I have help outside the building and I can get us out of here," Cole said.

"What about the others? The other women who are trapped here. What about them?"

Screw 'em. Cole thought. He was here to help his sister, not rescue a damn village like some hero. But before he could speak, Ainsley leaned forward and moved a book off her tablet screen. She tapped it twice and then tossed it to Cole. He caught it and stared at the screen. It was a list of a dozen women and their headshot photos. Names and information written next to each picture.

"You want me to help all these people escape too? I don't know Ains, that's—"

"Not escape." Ainsley looked up at him, sunlight striking her hazel eyes, making them shimmer like the glare of a jaguar hidden in the trees. "We're fighting back."

* * *

The individuals on Ainsley's list all attested to being abused by their spouses. Most were considered power couples of the city. There were two men on the list. Cole asked about them.

"Both of their wives have responded positively to in utero gene therapy, but it's the husband's sperm that's the problem." Ainsley said.

"Wait…so they can edit…that?"

Ainsley nodded. "Probably not a fun surgery for a man, but I'm a little short on sympathy when it comes to men and their reproductive organs and *pain*."

Cole nodded. "Okay, so it's abuse essentially from both sides."

"Correct."

"Why not go report them? Lawyer up and move out."

"Bring in the lawyers?" Ainsley laughed, "Right, if we did that, the Praetorians would be here in a heartbeat."

Praetorians. Cole thought, "Wait, Ainsley, the guards have already been here. They were here last night but gone when I got here in the early morning,"

Ainsley's eyes widened. "What? They were here? You're sure?"

"White electric-SUVs, grayish uniform—"

"That's them, dammit, okay, umm that's not good. They didn't come to this apartment, which means they must have visited one of the people on my list. Four of them live in Pylône Sept." Ainsley tapped each face on the tablet and sent a message to them. Moments later the responses all piled back in except for one, Colleen Broderick. Ainsley called her directly, the dial tone kept ringing out of the tablet. Cole and Ainsley sat patiently. "Colleen call me back ASAP," Ainsley said to the voicemail, and hung up.

"We didn't see them taking anyone with them and there's still some guards out front."

"Who's *we*?"

"Two colleagues I work with and a brilliant woman named Zelda. She's the one who hacked into the security feed and got me into that drone. She's back on the other side."

Ainsley nodded and stretched her arms in the air as if preparing for a dive. "I was afraid they'd catch on. Okay this means Colleen may still be in her apartment. Maybe they gave her a warning."

"Do they do that?"

"I don't know, sometimes I guess, or they take you to a holding cell in the center of town at Janus Tower. Or..." Ainsley's eyes began pooling again, then she stood. "I need to see her. Wait here. I'm going down there."

"No, they probably have guards outside her apartment."

Ainsley grunted with frustration and sat back down.

"How could they have found out?" Cole asked.

"They're masters at spy craft, stalking, making people disappear...someone must have spoken to the wrong person. Or their spouse found out. That's why I programmed this thing," Ainsley waved her tablet, "to only work when I hold it."

"Ains, how do you intend to fight back?"

She looked at her brother and grinned. "I want to expose these pricks. Martin, the Janus Corporation and their societal government officials; anyone who's behind the curtain destroying our lives. And I want this tech to be accessible to everyone, not just Crystalleans."

Cole considered this and knew where his place was before she even asked.

"You're the best computer engineer in the country. I know you're still upset about what happened in Boston but I need—we need your help."

"How do the other people in the city not know about this? You said it yourself that this is the *vision* of Crystalline. Surely everyone must know that they use gene editing tech to achieve this."

Ainsley shook her head. "Anything negative gets buried. People accept it because they have to. The influencer score is all that matters. Husband's DWIs, wives cheating with their yoga instructors, their teenager's misbehaviors… *failed* births. This is the city that was *built* off of the image of the perfect man and woman, and they intend to keep it that way and quietly cut away the '*extra fat*' as Martin refers to it."

"I see," Cole said in quiet shock.

"If we can get the message, the truth, plastered across the Janus social networks, people will see firsthand what's going on, and there's no controlling it after that. Just like the Pentagon Papers or Snowden's whistleblowing. We need a good ole fashion American exposé."

"What exactly are you going to show?"

Ainsley gave a weary look. "My medical records."

"But wouldn't that…"

"I'd be hunted down, yes. But I won't be the only one. The others said they'll release their medical records too. There'd be no stopping the deluge of damaging information. We just need to ensure it's seen and can stay up there."

Cole thought for a moment. Zelda told him that the Janus social network had effectively become the intranet of Crystalline. Its citizens wholeheartedly accepted the company's viewpoints and shut out all opposing thoughts. They'd effectively fed their users propaganda tailored to their specific interests. This was something governments and organizations tried to do for centuries; now, in a scathing case of irony, the people had done it to themselves. If Ainsley could crack into this fortified zeitgeist, she may be able to do irreversible damage. Similar to when the two Koreas reunited.

"So *this* is why you wanted me here? You know it's doing things like this is why I'm not allowed back in any university." Cole asked.

Ainsley looked at him and pursed her lips slightly. "You're the only one I know who could help," she whispered. "You're the only one."

Cole looked at her for a long time. He was getting upset with himself for not emphatically saying yes right away. This is *his* sister. Without family there's nothing. *But she did abandon the family*, he thought. The internal dialogue droned on until he stood and walked to the window. Looking down at the circuit board streets and highways cutting through the metallic cityscape, he wondered what damage this would do. He thought of historic uprisings and how they typically led to dramatic riots, burning cars, police and teargas. Was that possible here? Was it worth it? Cole was trying to bring himself to be compassionate about a mass of people; something he felt men of God could only do. The part of him that just wanted to grab Ainsley, reconnect with Duke and Rafiq, and get the hell out of here was still strong. He knew though there was the moral decision he had to make…and it wasn't running.

"Cole?"

He sighed with closed eyes. "Do you have a computer?" Cole said, turning to her.

A smile grew across her face. "I have this?" Ainsley held up the tablet. "I think there's a keyboard that connects to it somewhere."

Cole rolled his eyes. *Great, this'll be like fighting a bear with a ping-pong paddle,* he thought. He needed something with more power. "Does Martin have a system that's more substantial?"

Ainsley got up from the couch and motioned for him to follow. They walked down a white hallway, following the pattern glaze of the hickory floorboards, then entered what Cole presumed to be Martin's office. The office was immaculate. Leather-bound books sat perfectly together on high shelves that gleamed from the sunlight passing through the floor-to-ceiling windows. A koa wood desk stood on chrome legs, a chair tucked beneath it. Cole eyed the rig that was hidden behind the desk. It was an updated version of what Zelda had, an Orion-Tau MK 46 by the looks of it. Cole took a seat at Martin's chair and had the feeling a dog must get when it takes over the space of another's, a feeling of screw-you-this-is-my-domain-now pride.

"Password? And please don't tell me it's *password*," Cole asked.

"'Arjuna1010,' capital *A*," Ainsley replied.

Cole's fingers shot across the keyboard at a rapid pace. Two glass screens rose from the desk and powered on. A low hum protruded from beside Cole's feet. The Orion-Tau was powering up. He looked at his sister.

"If we do this," Cole paused. "There's no turning back."

Ainsley nodded with the fiercest glint in her eye. *That* was the look he remembered of his sister: compassionate, but tough as nails.

TWELVE

"Martin's due back here at four o'clock, correct?" Cole asked.

"Yes," Ainsley shuddered. "He and the doctor are making a house call." She checked her watch. It read a quarter to noon. Cole had been cycling through different screens, all showing coding terminals for the last three hours. He created various Janus profiles in order to penetrate their system.

"That's cutting it close. Even if I can break in, I don't think that would prevent Martin and this doctor from coming back to the apartment."

Ainsley nodded, biting her nail. "What about your guys, Dude and Rafiq?"

"*Duke* and Rafiq said they were going to try find a way in but—"

There was a knock at the front door. Cole's stomach sank and Ainsley gave a terrified look. The two left Martin's study and quietly headed for the foyer. Ainsley flipped on a security camera feed from her tablet and saw two men standing at the front door in oil-stained jumpers.

"Wait Cole, stop, what are you doing?"

Cole opened the door and the two men looked up from dirty hats and smirked. Rafiq spoke first. "We're here to fix the pipes." They both walked in and Ainsley shut the door quickly and locked it.

"I should've listened to Duke earlier. A plumber can go anywhere." Rafiq laughed.

Duke nodded and grinned.

They set down their toolboxes and took off the messy dark blue jumpers. Ainsley gave their Crystallean clothing an approving nod.

"I'm Ainsley Wainwright, Cole's sister," Ainsley said.

Duke took the end of her hand gently and smiled. Rafiq gave a shy wave, something he did in front of attractive women he met at bars. Cole grunted.

"No one followed you up here, right? Did you see any guards?" Cole asked.

"I sent Rafiq to go find a hardware store while I watched the guards patrol for the better part of an hour. We slipped into the building right between a lapse in their timing. The front desk was no problem," Duke said.

The server-bot zipped over to the two plumbers and produced glasses of cucumber water. Rafiq and Duke took the tall glasses and the bot hurried away back toward the kitchen.

Duke took a long sip. "Alright, so we're ready to go?"

Cole and Ainsley looked at each other, figuring who should tell them the story again. Cole could see the pain in her eyes. He gave an abridged version.

"Jesus, I'm so sorry," Duke said.

"I don't know what to say, that's just, just," Rafiq trailed off.

"Awful," Duke said. "And this Martin guy will be here in a couple of hours?"

Ainsley nodded.

"Well then, I can't wait to meet them, now that I have my tools," Duke said.

Cole looked up from the computer screens. "Let's hope it doesn't have to come to that. I feel that could bring the Crystalline Guard here pretty quickly."

"Not if we gag them," Rafiq said.

Cole shook his head and looked at Ainsley, pointing at her forearm. "Can you explain? I need to focus.

Ainsley held up her arm and pointed at the puffy incision scar. "RFID trackers can also monitor vital signs. Top brass members of the societal government have their vitals directly fed to the guards."

"We'll use that thing Zelda gave you," Rafiq said.

Cole was too deep in focus to respond, but gave a thumbs up. He wasn't about to share with everyone that each attempt to penetrate the internal servers of the Janus social network had failed. It was like playing chess against an opponent who got to move five pieces on every turn. Part of him, the pure rational side, hoped he couldn't break in. If that became the case, his only option would be to grab Ainsley and flee Crystalline. A sense of foreboding began to rise when he thought of the other people Ainsley showed him. Here were people that came to a new city to better their lives. It may have been based in vanity, but that's not inherently evil, is it? Cole remembered pride being one of the seven deadly sins and shrugged. He hated when his mind battled with itself.

Error flashed across the screen as another attempt failed.

Cole dropped his head to the keyboard muttering complex profanities. *Call her,* his mind urged. He didn't want to, though. Zelda had been too generous with her time. But he knew she could be the change agent here. She talked with ease about infiltrating Crystalline's system, like it was as simple as making pancakes. Plus she had an Orion-Tau, albeit an older model.

"You alright, Cole?" Duke asked.

Cole nodded and took out his phone.

"Zelda. I need your help. It's urgent. You may have to take the rest of the day off."

* * *

"Holy hell, I knew it was bad over there, but not like this," Zelda said after hearing Ainsley's backstory. "I can help, but I don't know Cole…the Janus corporation hires the best of the best. Breaking through their code walls is the holy grail for hackers. I've only skirted the edges of their system."

Cole said he understood and that she was the only person he could turn to for something like this. He added too that Ainsley would help foot the bill when she got out of there. That made Zelda's grin widen on the video screen of Cole's phone.

"A good cause and a good payday. Can't beat that. Alright, let's get to work."

Over the next two hours Cole and Zelda formed a position around the code walls of one of the Janus social networks with the URL of jsn.coffee; a small network for coffee aficionados. They began with a flurry of DDOS attacks to overwhelm and confuse the system, similar to the Blitzkrieg tactic used in the nascent throes of the Second World War. Then Zelda led a SQL-Injection attack on the central database that controlled the network. It felt like they were making progress, but the colossal force of the code's script kept morphing and defending.

Rafiq, Duke and Ainsley left Cole in the office alone. They were in the other room setting up the furniture so Martin and the doctor wouldn't see them at first.

"And then we'll grab his arm and deactivate the RFID tracker?" Rafiq asked for the second time, wanting to be sure of every step.

"Yes. It'll be fast but we'll have the jump," Duke said. "Don't screw this up."

"I won't."

Ainsley looked the clock on the wall. Martin was due back in ten minutes. He hadn't contacted her all day. She reminded herself this was normal during working hours. But she feared that he sensed her discomfort this morning. Wives are interlopers of their husband's minds, but today she wasn't getting a read.

"You really think your friends will pull through in sharing their medical records and stories to the public?" Rafiq asked Ainsley.

She turned to him with a cold glare. "The pain we've endured is far greater than whatever will happen publicly. It has to be done."

Rafiq nodded silently.

"Hey Ainsley?" Cole shouted from behind the closed door of the office. "Can you get in here please?"

Ainsley hurried, leaving Duke and Rafiq in the main room; they were being offered more food from the server-bot. Rafiq wondered if he could steal this *lil' fucker* as he admirably called it. He tried lifting the bot just to see and a tiny arm protruded from the center and zapped Rafiq with an electric shock, causing him to fall backward and yelp like a Chihuahua. Duke chuckled.

Inside the office stood a sweating but grinning Cole Wainwright. "We broke through, I think," he said. "Zelda's doing a runaround review to ensure we're not in some false system. But I think we did it. I can't keep it open long. Soon the code'll wise up and boot us out. What I'll need—"

The sound of the front door at the apartment beeped and the locks buzzed open. Ainsley and Cole looked at each other with confused terror. The clock read a quarter to four. Cole asked Zelda if she saw Martin on the external security screens.

"My eyes have been off it since we started getting deep in the code…they may have slipped by."

"Who the hell are you?" a voice said from the main room.

Ainsley looked like the air had been sucked from her lungs. Everything after that happened very fast.

* * *

When Martin walked into his apartment with Dr. Geary he saw two gruff looking men standing in his living room. One of them looked like a real-life Goliath. The other one was leaner but had a fierce look in his eyes, like an agitative varmint. The Goliath had his hands leaning on the edge of the couch, which for some reason had been turned around so the other end faced the door.

"Who the hell are you?" Martin asked.

That's when Rafiq threw a crystal scotch tumbler in the air toward Dr. Geary. Both Martin and the doctor's eyes followed the gleaming glass in the air like tennis spectators. Duke sprang forward in an explosive lunge pushing the couch at full speed across the room like an upholstered battering-ram. The doctor and Martin let out wails when the couch connected to their knees and pinned them against the front door. The crystal glass was caught by the server-bot and then it scurried away, as if it had been programmed to look out for marital spats. Rafiq leaped on the couch and punched Dr. Geary in the jaw while Duke calmly but swiftly made his way to Martin, striking his throat with the area of his hand between index finger and thumb.

Ainsley and Cole ran into the room to see Martin, struggling for air, like some sick alien who had landed on a planet with an inhospitable atmosphere. Dr. Geary lay unconscious with blood trickling from his nose and mouth. Duke looked over his back and saw the two Wainwrights staring at the scene with shock.

"The RFID trackers. Come on, we don't have a lot of time," Duke said to Rafiq, who took out the device. Rafiq scanned both their arms and the device pinged a low beep with a green light. "Good. Now grab his feet."

"Cole…hey Cole, the code is closing!" Zelda shouted from the office.

Cole ran back to the desk. Ainsley followed. On the screens a series of cascading terminal lines flowed steadily, countermeasures were fighting against them. Cole went back on the offensive and looked at the video phone. Zelda was scrolling through different sections of the code. That split second of looking at the phone made Cole miss something and just like that he was locked out. An alert pinged on Zelda's screen.

"You're out?" Zelda said, her eyes not leaving the screen.

"Goddammit. Yes. Let me try something else."

"Don't bother Cole. You've agitated it too much. The code is in full defense mode. Any more tampering they'll be able to track the location of that rig," Zelda said.

Cole pounded the desk, causing picture frames and pens to jitter. "You're right."

"I think I can still get in… I'm deep inside, one more barrier to go." Zelda seemed to be holding her breath. Then she hissed out a long sigh. "In. Give me the Ainsley file."

Cole looked up at Ainsley for a last second of approval. She nodded. "Sending the files over now," Cole said. Zelda gave a quick nod and wiped sweat from her brow. She was in a black tank top now. The tendons in her arms danced in the light.

"Done," Zelda said, sitting back in her chair, the two front feet leaving the ground slightly as she pushed against the desk. "The story, the files, are out there. It'll be distributed to every screen in that whole city," Zelda said. A grin slowly grew from both sides of her dimpled cheeks. She was, rightfully so, the first person to succeed in breaking into the Janus corporation's system. The grin slowly waned like gray clouds against a moon. It was clear she'd started thinking of the implications.

"We covered our tracks," Cole said.

Zelda nodded. "No stopping it now. The die has been cast…"

Ainsley left the room.

"You did great work. I can't thank you enough," Cole said.

"Team effort. You're not too bad yourself. When you're back I think we should grab a drink. Sound good?" She looked into the screen, right into Cole's sea green eyes.

"I'd love that. I—" Cole heard muffled screams emanating from the living room. He jumped from his chair and ran to the commotion.

Ainsley was being restrained by Duke. Martin and Dr. Geary were tied up in Barcelona chairs. Their arms were strapped to the ends of the chairs, leaving their chests and bellies exposed. Rafiq thought it was necessary, for some odd reason, to remove their shirts. Both of the men were awake now with gagged mouths, and their eyes darting back and forth like pinballs. Sticking out of Dr. Geary's thigh was a fountain pen.

Cole was speechless. His sister's eyes had changed somehow, to the glare of a predator. She hissed at the two bound men, "You're both going to burn. You and your city." Duke brought Ainsley to another room to help her calm down.

Martin's stone-gray eyes were staring at the fountain pen which now leaked a mix of blue and red fluids onto the floor from the doctor's thigh. He motioned to Cole who walked over and removed the gag.

"What did she tell you?" Martin said.

"I know everything, you prick. I know about the in utero gene therapy, the abortions, the—"

"How many did she tell you about? How many times?"

Cole was confused. "Three or so; it takes a real monster to do something like this."

Martin shook his head. "It only happened once. One time. And it was *her* idea. Check the doc's briefcase."

Cole motioned to Rafiq to retrieve it.

Zelda's distant voice sounded from the office. Cole couldn't tell what she was saying. He ignored it and opened the briefcase. A screen lit up and beamed a laser keyboard on the bottom. Martin gave the password and the screen opened to Ainsley Wainwright-Spiros's official medical records. Cole read them twice, ignoring the banter from Ainsley's room and the pleas from Zelda. *This cannot be right*, he thought.

"These are fake," Cole said dismissively, not believing his own statement.

Martin shook his head again, frustrated at the blatant stupidity around him. "She's *lying* Cole. Your sister is not what she seems."

"Cole!" Zelda screamed now. "Cole!"

He left Martin there with Rafiq and returned to the office. Zelda had a look of panic on the screen.

"Ainsley's files…I didn't review them before posting but…" Zelda stared at her terminal screen and then back at the files. "These are forgeries, digital forgeries. They're good but not great."

The fear sunk into Cole deeply, to his bones, like falling into a snowbank. All of his joints and tendons tightened. His tongue went dry as he processed everything.

"Cole, your sister is lying. This is all a ruse. Why would she do this Cole? Why?"

Commotion sounded outside, a great uproar, one that could only be felt at a stadium, bellowed from the streets below. The giant billboards that draped the lower halves of buildings was Ainsley's story. Her video was different from the one she'd shown Cole. In this video she wore a uniform of some sort, and a dark-skinned woman stood beside her.

"Zelda, I can't hear what the video is. Are you getting any of this?"

"Hang on." Zelda raised the volume of her speakers and it played through the phone to Cole.

Ainsley's voice had a commanding tone: "*…and now we rise up, together as New Crystalleans, reborn from the ash of the tyrants that has poisoned this great city. You've seen what they've done to us. The societal government is stripping mothers of their babies and commanding our way of life. This cannot stand. The tech must be shared with the rest of the world. Crystalline must fall for that to happen. Rise up, have no fear, for there are more of you than them. Let's not forget why we moved to this great city. We are the superior-beings. We will take what's ours. We will share this to all that need it. We will save humanity…*"

An agreeable roar bellowed from the streets. Cole looked back at Zelda, who was holding her mouth with both hands; a motion reserved for when you've broken something irreplaceable, like antique China, or an Impressionist's oil painting. But Zelda had done something far worse. Lives would be lost. Buildings would burn. Zelda was the facilitator.

"Your…sister. She has started a coup."

THIRTEEN

Bedrooms in Pylône Sept were designed to be a sanctuary for intimacy, fertility and love. The walls were higher than the other rooms, and brilliant bacchanal frescos were painted along the cone shape ceilings. The beds were elevated several feet off the ground like an exaggerated altar. The interior lighting changed throughout the day in accordance with the sun. Since it was approaching evening the lights were shifting from neutral to amber when Cole entered Ainsley's bedroom. He didn't notice the details of the room. Too much had happened.

Ainsley stood by the floor to ceiling windows, looking down on the chaos below. Her video message replayed across the colossal billboards and augmented projection screens. It played across the Janus social networks. Every Crystallean had received the message and shared it, creating an unstoppable network effect, like a plague permeating through a reservoir. Duke sat beside her in a velvet tufted chair that was too big for his frame. Duke, fist to chin, hunched over taking the pose of *The Thinker*. His ice blue eyes darted up at Cole.

Duke's mouth opened to speak but he said nothing, continuing to think. Cole gave a quiet nod to him and approached Ainsley. She saw his reflection in the glass and turned, smiling like Simón Bolívar.

"We did it, Cole," Ainsley said.

Pent up rage and anger, the kind he felt only when he was a boy, shot off like steam through an overclocked radiator. "What the fuck is wrong with you? You're going to get us all killed. You lied to me. I risked my life to get here, I asked these men help *you*. I—"

"You did help me Cole. You did. Look at this. For the first time, we may have a real shot at achieving the destinies that are set for us."

"Destiny? Destiny? Did you really just say that? Is it to create the übermensch? Fulfill some delusional prophecy?" Cole shouted, his face growing red.

"I believe that we will all rise as a species," Ainsley said in calm tone. "What has been built here cannot stay in Crystalline. It must be shared with the world. By getting the people out of here, sharing their stories, their knowledge, Janus will have no choice but to share their tech too."

Cole threw his hands in the air and began pacing around the room. Ainsley returned to looking through the window, reveling in it. Duke got up from the low velvet chair and put his hand on Cole's shoulder.

"I understand you're upset," Duke said. "But I think this was the right thing to do, even if it meant being fooled."

Cole stepped away from Duke as if he were a frisky stranger at a bus stop. "What? Duke? You of all people—"

"I've seen plenty of societies when I was in the military. This one is no different, albeit with a few technical advances. Societies need to have a goal to work towards. America is capitalism, freedom, excess. Some other societies are barbaric dictatorships that thrive off of the masses. History is littered with the skeletons of societies that tried to take too much out of those with too few. Republics need a moral goal to survive." Duke paused and looked over at Ainsley. "You may not know it; but this woman here might be the force that changes this plutocracy into a functioning republic."

Cole said nothing. His anger began to fade as the logic worked its way through his mind like a new stream over a dry riverbed. Seeking. Imbuing. Absorbing.

"But this editing of the genome… people aren't computers you can tweak. These vessels have souls…" Cole trailed off, shaking his head and looking at the ground.

"It's absurd to think about it, trust me on that. The most sophisticated tool I use is a twelve inch monkey wrench," Duke said. "But…if I could've removed that part of my mom's gene pool or whatever you call it, to get rid of her thyroid cancer, you bet your ass I'd do that. And if I ever had kids, I'd for sure never want them to be at risk for it."

Cole nodded.

Duke continued, "What if this tech could be shared with the world? What if these souls could *thrive*? What then? It could be like Silicon Valley in the 1980s or Britain in the 1840s. This could be the new cradle of civilization."

Cole looked up at Duke. He could see Ainsley with her back to them but nodding, nearly ready to shout out an *amen!*

"You think a brute like me just sits there all day with his tools thinking about pipe fittings and steak?" Duke said with a coy grin.

They both laughed. It was true. Cole had seen dozens of paperbacks scattered about Duke's bulldozer cockpit; names like Aurelius, Seneca, Tocqueville, Jefferson, and Jung were printed on the covers. Ainsley walked over to the two men. She looked at Cole with a *I hope you understand* look.

"We need your help, Cole," Ainsley said.

"I'm still pissed at you."

"I can live with that if you help us."

Ainsley was about to shake Cole's hand when the entire room went dark. The continuous pink neon hue from city was still visible in the evening light. It reflected into the dark bedroom. Duke, Ainsley and Cole looked around and noticed the entire apartment had lost power. Outside, the city of Crystalline began losing power block by block. The city, like the apartment in Pylône Sept, was silent. It felt like the forbidding calm of a fast-approaching storm.

* * *

The green lines of drone traffic dotted across the slate sky of a dead city. Electro buses, monorails and autonomous taxis stood idle. Pedestrians were using their phones as flashlights to navigate around the city. Judging from the rhythm of movement, a panic below was brewing.

Ainsley checked her watch. "We're going to need to get out of the Pylône before the guards show up. I'm sure they've already been dispatched."

"What about the guards outside?" Cole asked.

Ainsley shook her head. "We'll have to risk it. C'mon, let's go."

Duke followed Ainsley out of the room. Cole stared out the window for a moment, then went to the living room. Rafiq looked nervous when they entered.

"The doctor passed out. He's breathing, but it's shallow, I don't know if he's gonna have a heart attack or what," Rafiq said.

Ainsley shrugged. "He couldn't handle the pain. What a chump." She patted the cheek of the doctor twice and looked at Martin, who was weary eyed; the adrenaline had faded. Ainsley removed the gag. "Goodbye my love." She kissed him once on the lips and replaced the gag. He started moaning, trying to speak.

"We're not bringing him?" Duke asked.

"No, his bosses will torture him more than I could ever stomach," Ainsley answered. She checked her watch. "Time to go."

The crew followed Ainsley to the front door and down the hall toward a service elevator still running off the building's backup generator. Inside, Cole asked where they were going, Ainsley didn't answer, warning that there could be microphones in the elevator. They rode in silence. Awful Muzak played gently. The doors opened in the underground parking garage. Each of them turned on flashlights. A collection of high-end autonomous sports cars sat with their hoods facing out, gleaming. An older looking car sat in the corner under a dusty cover.

Ainsley pulled the cover off to reveal an old Porsche 911, the ones you used to be able to drive manually. She took out a key and unlocked the car, then she tossed her bag in the trunk. Ainsley looked up and saw Rafiq, Duke and Cole staring at her.

"We're traveling in this antique? We'll be seen immediately," Cole said.

Ainsley smirked. "We're not going on the roads."

"Does this thing fly or something?" Rafiq asked.

Ainsley laughed. "Get in. Rafiq and Cole in the back; big guy up front."

After some maneuvering, they piled into the old German sports car. Its shocks creaked as the passengers settled in. Ainsley turned the key and the yellow headlamps came alive. She pumped the gas twice, depressed the clutch and fired up the air-cooled engine. The exhaust roar made Cole jump. Ainsley reached into the center console and pulled out a pair of leather driving gloves the color of cognac. She smiled at Cole in the rearview and tossed it in gear. They headed through the gloomy parking garage. It felt like a cave on an alien planet.

Ainsley approached the exit sign, but turned away from it. They headed for the lower levels of the parking garage. Deeper underground they moved beneath Pylône Sept. Finally they reached the lowest level, floor sub-9D. The Porsche came up to an area that had been walled off by a floor-to-ceiling chain-linked fence. It seemed to be where maintenance equipment was held. Gardening and commercial cleaning tools were scattered about.

The Porsche rolled to a stop. Ainsley pulled the handbrake up and stepped out. "Wait here," she said, leaving her door open. Her boots echoed off the concrete walls.

Duke looked back at Cole. "You notice anything odd about those tools?"

Cole squinted and nodded. "They look older than the city itself. No one uses rakes here, the landscape-bots and external vacuums pick all that up."

"Yeah, that's what I was thinking too."

Ainsley took a brass key from her bra and unlocked the double-door fence, tossing both open. Then she began moving the tools, lawnmowers, tarp and plywood out of the way. Soon Cole was able to make out a void beyond his sister, a dark void where light didn't enter. After a few minutes Ainsley hopped back in the car and carefully drove forward toward the previously fenced off area. The yellow headlamps illuminated the path ahead of them.

"Well, I'll be damned," Duke said, chuckling.

Before them was a hollowed out hole in the wall matching the shape and height of the Porsche. Ainsley carefully feathered the throttle to move the front of the Porsche through the tunnel entrance and the exhausted responded angrily. Once they were past the fence gate, Ainsley hopped out again and closed them from the inside. She locked them, stuck the brass key in the lock and broke the key within it. Then she moved all the equipment back together and covered the hole up from the tunnel side with the tarp and plywood.

The Porsche drove on through the damp tunnel. Cole noticed it taking a larger shape and realized they were eventually back in a hyperloop tunnel. He asked where they were going and Ainsley grinned. "To see the woman who started it all."

Tossing the Porsche into high gear, she hammered the throttle and accelerated through the dark metallic tunnel.

* * *

Cruising speed within the tunnel produced a monotonous hum similar to the old Cessna their father Rex owned when Cole and Ainsley were young. The constant gnawing through the air eventually becomes tranquil enough to sleep to. Cole would always get irritated at his sister when she'd fall asleep on those plane rides across the Midwest. "*You're missing it*," he'd moan, but soon too Cole would be asleep as he watched the green and gold plains roll on forever interrupted only by roads and rivers.

It felt like they'd been driving in a straight line for the better half of the last hour. However, they were on a slight bend, wrapping around Crystalline and heading to the other side of the city. The service tunnel was similar to the one Cole used to break into the city, but Rafiq assured him it wasn't the same. He'd never been underground this long before with no breaks in the tunnel, no junctions, no access points, just a long tube like the barrel of a bent rifle.

Ainsley kept checking her rearview mirror. Cole shuddered. If they were caught here there'd be nowhere to go. Porsche may have once been the king of the road, but the equipment the Crystalline Guard carried was superior. The electric-SUVs were silent. Cole started to wonder if they *were* being tailed; all they'd have to do is shut off their lights and follow the gnawing hum and fading red tail-lamps.

"No one's behind us Cole," Ainsley said. "No one yet."

Cole heard the throttle increase slightly and the gnawing pitch change.

"Where are we going?" Cole asked.

"To see the others; the mailer-drone maintenance tower in the Utility Zone."

"Where's that?" Cole asked. He tugged on his seatbelt like a toddler with a security blanket.

"The Utility Zone is the part of the city where everything gets built and repaired. It's where all the landscaping-bots live, the drones, buses, anything more mechanically advanced than a toothbrush. Like one big command center for the Janus corporation's tools."

"Hey," Rafiq said. "Wouldn't that place be guarded then? What the hell are you doing, girl?"

"First, don't call me *girl*; second, yes it will be heavily guarded, but they mainly patrol the outer limits of the area. No sense patrolling within, at least that's what the intel told us. It makes sense. Would you want to patrol the outside of a bank or the inside of the janitor's closet?" Ainsley said.

A silence lingered and the gnawing hum continued. Duke, who was holding on to the roof grab handle, looked over at Ainsley. He went to speak but then turned straight ahead and watched the yellow headlights widen the path in front of them. Ainsley downshifted and the exhaust whined higher and popped twice. They slowed to a massive interior space. It felt like they were in the bottom of a great silo where ICBMs used to live.

In block lettering the along the inner walls it read: JUNCTION U98-A-003. The Porsche came to a stop at the center of the junction point. Six other tunnels fed through here. Catwalks circled above at ten stories high. Cranes and other mechanical arms jutted out at various heights of the tall silo structure.

"This where they launch the space shuttle?" Duke asked.

"Bingo," Ainsley said. "No launches are on the manifest for the next couple of months, hence the emptiness."

Duke shrugged. "Can I get out of this clown car now?"

A smile grew across Ainsley's face, her soft skin reflected in the dash's light, which gave her eyes a sparkle. "Hang on a little longer, Duke. I have to see which elevator we'll need to get to." Ainsley scanned ahead of her. "There, Door 45-XI," She stuck the car in gear and drove up to a metal door that opened from the center horizontally. Giant steel plates disappeared and an empty holding cell revealed itself. The light beside the door glowed green and a buzz sounded. Ainsley drove the car within the elevator and the steel doors slammed shut like a trap. Another buzz sounded and Ainsley shut off the car. All they could hear now was the circuitous sound of the elevator motor.

Cole looked at Rafiq, who had his eyes squeezed shut. He was praying in Spanish.

After two minutes of lifting, a slit of light broke through the elevator doors. It was moonlight, a harvest moon. The haunting light made the interior of the car pale gray. They were back above ground and climbing. An abrupt halt made the occupants jump in their seats. The steel doors opened slowly and Ainsley fired up the Porsche again. The yellow headlamps revealed something horrifying: legs, dozens of legs.

As the Porsche slowly climbed from the elevator the headlamps moved upward slightly enough to cast a light on the row of people the legs belong to. As if choreographed, they all put their right arms in front of the beam of light. Ainsley drove toward them, then turned the car slightly and shut the engine off. Darkness returned and the people were gone. Cole looked around and noticed a small red LED lighting on the ceiling, night vision, he figured. Closing his eyes, he opened them again, forcing his body to adjust to the dim lights. Soon the people returned and they were all walking toward the car. Fear grew in his chest. This was it. They were caught, they were—

"Ainsley?" said a friendly woman's voice.

Ainsley laughed, unbuckling her seatbelt and leaping from the car. "Saba!" she said, running over to the woman. They embraced for a few moments and looked back at the three men tiredly climbing from the car.

Cole walked over to his sister and saw a slender woman with thick black hair and deep maple eyes looking at him. She grinned widely and her teeth were brilliantly white like foamed milk.

"Cole, this is Saba, the woman who started it all."

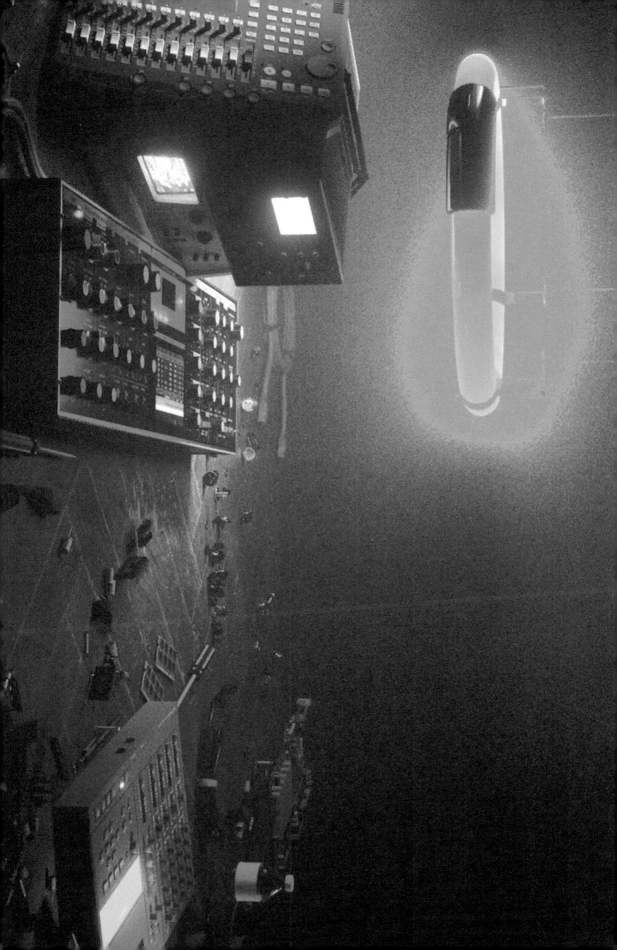

FOURTEEN

Saba Nazari spent most her life in Swiss boarding schools. There were times she'd visit home in Bahrain, but even then the majority of her time was dedicated to the work at the Mosque. Which meant that up until nineteen years old Saba spent the waking hours of the day guided by instruction in religion, education and etiquette. Her father, Ekram, didn't believe all the rules must be followed. His daughter was to be treated with dignity and equality, regardless of what the Quran said. Ekram was the kindling of Saba's rebellious spirit. Though it was never against her family or even the Imams, but the ones holding the true purse strings of society: private companies. In the twenty first century, that was where power was made manifest. Centuries prior, it had been the temples, cathedrals, and mosques that held the power. From the time she was a little girl with hair as dark as coal she grew obsessed with power.

Tonight she had never felt so close to it. Standing in this cold tower within the Utility District of Crystalline she felt the alluring titillation power produces. Now facing this man Ainsley had spoken of made her almost giddy. Saba felt warm, as if this man's potential energy could produce real heat. She stepped closer and shook Cole's hand. His intense sea green eyes made her feel she was the only one in the room. Attraction was real, yes, but it was something different; the brilliance this man contained was exactly what Saba knew would make this city fall. She took a step closer and kissed his cheek.

He smiled and said something, but Saba couldn't hear, she was lost in dreams of the future, imagining herself at the helm of the world's most advanced city. Saba noticed Ainsley looking at her too, along with the two men that climbed out of the Porsche.

"Forgive me, I misheard you," Saba said.

"I was asking if you're really the brains of this operation," Cole said.

Saba felt ripped from the dream state by this statement. *Brains.* What a tawdry use of words to describe *her* and what she'd done to Crystalline, and what she *would* do. Saba dropped Cole's hand and took a step back from everyone. The people still stared at her. One of them looked like a silverback gorilla and had the brow to prove it. Saba put on the act that she'd practiced since she was a little girl.

Fawning a laugh to lighten the mood, mainly hers, she said, "Why yes I am. But it wouldn't have worked without everyone's help." Saba raised both arms like a jazz singer standing centerstage. "And your marvelous work too, Cole."

Cole folded his arms. Saba could see Duke and Rafiq had done the same. A small phalanx now stood in front of her and the people she was trusting her life with. *Have I really misread the situation this poorly?* she thought.

"I was coerced into this predicament; I didn't volunteer. Neither did Duke and Rafiq."

Ah, the gorilla has a name of his own, Saba mused. She tried catching herself being snooty. Saba could be devastatingly hurtful if she needed to be, another learning from boarding with the Swiss. But she knew diplomatic action and compromise was the only way forward. Saba decided that direct logic was the best tactic for this situation. Clearing her throat, she spoke confidently. "I see, well, it seems you're here now, which should indicate you've found our cause worthy of your time."

"Yeah well, the toothpaste is already out of the tube," Cole said.

Toothpaste? Saba hated idioms and didn't understand why Americans used them so much. She smiled powerfully at Cole and turned slightly to have the red lighting accentuate the subtle curves in her figure. She saw all three of the men's shoulders soften, albeit slightly, and then she walked beside Ainsley. "Your sister and I have been working on this for months. Once we saw the potential, it had to be seized. We're at an inflection point in history. Only now can we make this leap and change the course of humanity's future forever."

"Ah huh, sounds like every startup I interned at," Cole remarked.

Saba scoffed. Ready to attack.

"But you're right," Cole said, rubbing his neck. "I see the path and the way this city is heading. It would be wrong for all of these advancements to remain private. Plus, the way they treat their citizens is obviously horrible. It's more akin to the old North Korea then to an American city. They do want to make other cities too, right?"

Saba smiled. *He does understand.*

"I wanted to let you know we're not happy about the sudden on-boarding to your team," Cole said.

"Fair enough. I promise there will be no surprises," Saba said.

"Fuckin' doubt that," Rafiq said.

Saba ignored the man. He clearly established his role on the totem pole, and it wasn't above the tree-line.

"Come inside," Saba said, motioning to a walled off conference room in the loft. Soft light emitted from beneath the doors and the smell of dumplings and umami spice began to fill the air. "We'll eat first and then discuss what's to come."

"You're confident no one will find this place?" Cole asked.

Saba nodded. "We have lookouts, plus, the Crystalline Guards are scouring Pylône Sept right now. There's enough time to dine with civility before next steps are made."

Cole noticed that all of a sudden he was famished. Saba took his arm and walked him toward the doors like a girlfriend wrangling a new man to show to her friends. Saba Nazari always got what she wanted.

* * *

The conference room looked like a sad blend of a strategy office within the Pentagon and a tired tax accountant's practice outside Omaha. Charts, maps and timetables were pinned to corkboard. A white stained coffeemaker stood nearby a mess of spilled sugar and creamer packets. Construction equipment lay about. There weren't any windows and a long orange electrical cord ran out underneath the door toward a generator that powered two construction lights set on sawhorses in the corner. Next to the lights were a few metal pots simmering, steam danced above. Rafiq grabbed a bowl and helped himself first.

Cole took a plate with bread and dumplings and walked toward the center conference table. On the table was an old laptop that looked like a clamshell. A few tablets lay nearby on charging plates. Cole wished they had an Orion-tau system somewhere, but this seemed to be it. *All the computing power of an elementary school.* Cole noticed the incision scars on everyone's arms, similar to Ainsley's, but cleaner.

Several newspapers were neatly displayed vertically against a whiteboard, like how doctors used to display x-rays. Red annotations and circles were on each page. Cole walked over to this without saying anything. *The New York Times, San Francisco Chronicle* and the *Chicago Tribune* had been displayed high on the board; beneath them were what looked like exact duplicates, same issue, same dates, but something was off. Cole examined in silence, ignoring the other people who were filing into the room. *The paragraphs are maligned.* Cole snapped his fingers and looked back at Saba who held a small grin.

"You see it don't you?" she asked.

Cole smiled. "They're not the same. The articles are covering identical issues, but the reporting…" Cole turned back and read the first two paragraphs on the *Chicago Tribune* and the duplicate below. "It's wrong. They're telling two different stories."

Saba nodded. "Very good. This is something Eliza noticed when she snuck out of Crystalline on a fact-finding mission." A red head woman with a freckled nose sat in the far end of the room, staring at a tablet. She looked up to wave at Cole.

"Newspapers?"

"People clutch nostalgia like religion. Thankfully, people still want newspapers. Makes sense too. No reason to stare at a screen all day. But we started to see the newspapers that Crystalleans have delivered to their apartments and offices, the lower ones," Saba motioned to the row with all the red annotations across the text, "are sometimes different than what's being reported outside Crystalline. Which means that Janus sees it fit to change the news from the *outside world* so it fits their narrative. And vice-versa of course. No one outside Crystalline is aware of how dire the city is."

"That's some Soviet-level thinking," Duke muttered as he took a seat in a swivel chair.

"Control the narrative," Saba said. "It's what tyrannical governments, hell even democracies to some extent, do their people. Eliza, myself and Ainsley here had started noticing strange practices after the first year of living in Crystalline. Then the in utero testing started… and that's when it all began to go sideways. Janus made a policy where your social ranking drops every minute you're outside Crystalline. It sounds crazy but it's an incentive powerful enough to keep people within the walls. Only approved Crystalleans can actually *leave* the city without repercussions. Since then, we've been building up evidence and researching everything Janus has been doing."

"To what end? There's no court you can show it to," Cole said.

"There's the press, the real press, outside these walls. There are still people that can get the truth out," Saba said.

Rafiq started laughing. "You think those news organization are any better? They've been bought and paid for." He took a bite into a dumpling, disregarding the mess he made.

Saba scowled at him, "We're not aiming for them; it's the ones who have tribes of their owns, the thought leaders, podcasters, writers; the ones with real followers. *They* will be our disciples. Their tribes listen to them. If we can get the truth to enough people, it can flood the collective consciousness of the country. When truth gains sustainable velocity, there's nothing that can stop it. That's its beauty."

A silence enveloped the room.

Saba looked at her team and the three latest additions. "Can you at least see the rationale here, Cole?" she asked.

Cole shrugged and swallowed another dumpling. "Yes… I mean it makes sense. Janus needs to keep everyone in order; they practically have the gestapo out there in the streets. It's their motives I cannot understand. They have money, power, tech, great minds…what is the end goal for them controlling their populous?"

"Compliance. So they can garner more power, money, minds, and tech," Saba answered.

"But why?"

"To colonize Mars, who the hell knows? It doesn't matter. We, *you*, Cole, have finally hit their Achilles heel. The beast isn't invincible. But they won't remain dark forever. The power will come back on and the guards will be out for blood. That's why I'm asking for your help. Not just for Ainsley's sake, but the sake of the half-million Crystalleans that need your help. They need to know the truth. The world needs to know…" Saba paused. "It's wrong they're keeping all this advanced tech to themselves when it can better the lives of humanity. Plus it sets a dangerous precedent. Janus isn't the only powerful company out there. Think of the domino effect. What if the banks decide to open their own cities?"

"It's called Manhattan, sweetheart," Rafiq said.

"Fair point. But the over-extending reach, the power these companies have, it's something that most people just don't seem to be concerned about. Governmental checks and balances are pure fiction now. Ever since the Nordic Wars, the Federal Government have been weakened so heavily…" Saba trailed off, exacerbated by pleading her point.

Cole understood and she was probably right, but he then thought of non-capitalist countries he'd visited. Ones where there was hardly any production. They were desolate wastelands. He considered this and figured westerners tolerate monopoly, even exploitation and abuse from companies to maintain the ideal of freedom. *"Golden handcuffs get tighter every year."* Cole remembered his mother once saying that after coming home from a long day at work. Even at eight years old Cole seemed to have the capacity to appreciate the home he occupied. Heat came on with the press of a button, there was hot water (which became luke-warm after Ainsley's twenty-two minute showers), the refrigerator, the La-Z-Boy recliner…the comfort elements, Maslow and his fucking needs, these corporations knew how to fulfill them. He then remembered the day that same company his mother had worked at for three decades fired her. A benevolent master until it changes its mind.

"I'm a capitalist," Cole stated. "But there comes a point where companies reach too far and act like plutocrats. We'll help you, Saba. But you have to promise us that—"

The door opened suddenly and the server-bot came into the room with drinks. Saba looked around confused. "You get that thing working again Eliza?"

Eliza shook her head and walked over toward it. She called outside the room to the few others that were keeping watch by the windows. "Hey, you guys fix the server-bot?"

"We assumed you did," said a voice from the window-wall.

Eliza looked back at the bot. Its headlight eye sensor turned red and she swore she saw the machine smile. That's when everything went white as a flash-bang from within it detonated.

Rafiq spent most of his teens and early-twenties in nightclubs and concert halls. Girls, drugs and drinks were fun, but the music, he held an insatiable urge to *feel* the music course through him. There had been plenty of occasions during that time where he became so inebriated his nerves stopped sending signals to him. Once he took what he thought was an ecstasy pill, but was instead ketamine. He fell into a stupor beside a great speaker in the Bowery Ballroom in the heart of Manhattan. A tired emergency room nurse said he'd ruptured his right eardrum. Rafiq was at the clubs the following weekend. To him the pain was worth it; he could handle the pain so long as the music was good.

The flash-bang grenade that detonated inside the conference room felt like the amalgam of sound and bass he'd absorbed throughout his entire party-fueled life. It hit all in one second. The pain was remarkable. He could feel the pulse in his temples and the beat of his heart. He lay there, blinking furiously to scrape the white from his eyes, thinking this was it, this was the end of Rafiq. One eye was able to see the others laying on the ground. *At least I won't die alone*, he figured as he shut his eyes again and listened to the faint tea-kettle ring that steamed somewhere far away, perhaps in another realm.

Rafiq didn't know when it happened, but soon he was being dragged. The Holy Ghost had selected him and he was being shepherded to the great beyond. A feeling of immense peace came over him. Rafiq smiled warmly. He was to see his family again, and when he got to heaven he'd—Rafiq's shoulder struck a desk leg. Opening his eyes, through blurry whitish vision he saw ceiling tile above. The carpet underneath him burned his skin raw. *Satan?*

There was the immediate feeling again of lightness as he was tossed over the side of a desk onto three other bodies. *The pit of the dead. I'm in hell.* Cold fear crept in. He saw the man next to him was Cole. Ainsley lay nearby, not moving either. Great guttural noises wretched from far away. This confirmed it. *I'm in hell, h-e-double hockey sticks,* as he remembered saying as a boy. Rafiq let the fear take him over, the sweet release, and he went into a deep terror-filled sleep.

On the other side of the conference room, Duke had grabbed hold of a sledgehammer near the sawhorses. He tossed the nearby people behind the overturned conference table and waited for the assailants to arrive. Duke could hear the shuffle of boots and their radios crackling static in the darkness. This gave him a second to shake off the sting of the flash-bang. His Marine instincts kicked in when he saw that little server-bot turn red. He covered his ears and sank his face into his lap. It wasn't one-hundred percent effective, but gave him a fighting chance.

The first guard to enter the smoky conference room was about the size of Duke. The sledgehammer swung smooth like a baseball player's swing and hit straight to the man's sternum. It sounded like a stack of textbooks striking the ground from a twenty story building. A deep *thunk,* and then the guard collapsed. His heart stopping in between beats.

Duke kicked the door shut and ran for cover behind the conference table where the unconscious team lay stirring. The Crystalline Guard shredded the door with bullets. Duke watched Rafiq get nicked by a ricochet, and it seemed to resurrect the man. Duke waited for a break in the gunfire and drew his .357 from the small of his back. Resting it atop of the lip of the table he fired two rounds into the wall, to the left and right of the door. A moment passed and he heard two bodies collapse. Duke repeated the shots but this time wider. The first was answered by nothing, but the second shot made one of them call out something in pain.

Duke took the opportunity to advance back toward the door and retrieve the weapon the Crystalline Guard with the collapsed chest held. A Beretta U22. Duke checked the clip and saw it was fully loaded. He grabbed the sledgehammer and smashed open the door, then he tossed the hammer outside. The guards began shooting the hammer in the darkness while Duke peaked out to see three guards in the muzzle-fire. He returned fire with the Beretta. Duke watched each of the men fall; one of them had a leaky skull. Duke took cover again and waited several minutes until he exited the conference room with his flashlight on. Six Crystalline Guards lay dead just feet from the door. By the window, Duke noticed two of Saba's men with open throats. He grimaced and looked away out toward the cursed city.

Crystalline.

Duke shook his head in astonishment at what had transpired over the last twenty-four hours. He continued to stare at the dark city; the power had yet to return. He heard people stirring from the conference room and went to return but saw something out of the corner of his eye, a red glare. Far in the distance he could see the Janus Tower. Usually it glowed white amongst the pinkish neon hue of the city, but this was different. The Janus Tower had turned a shade of blood orange. From the bottom, Duke marveled at the light rising to take the entire tower.

Instinct pulled him away from the window. If the Crystalline Guard knew their location, there would be reinforcements heading here right now. He hurried to the conference room where some members of the group were pulling themselves up out of their daze. Cole had a bloody nose and was unconscious. Ainsley was trying to wake him. Duke knelt beside Saba, who lay unconscious too. He set a hand on her bony shoulder and two maple eyes opened up at him, like looking down an autumn road in November. She seemed to be fine, as if she were stirred from a prolonged nap. Her brow furrowed away its simple beauty and she gripped her temples. Duke rubbed her shoulder and she pursed her lips and then smiled, mouthing, "Thank you."

"We need to get out of here. Tell me you have some sort of Plan…B or C?" Duke said.

Saba nodded, getting to her feet. "It was only a matter of time. We need to get everyone to the gates of the city."

Duke felt relief warm him like towels from a dryer. *We're getting out of the nightmare.*

Saba shook her head as if she had telepathically uncovered Duke's thoughts. "No, I mean *everyone.* At least those who will believe in our cause. We want the people to leave this city to tell their story. The curtain has been pulled back on Janus, the people can see they now have a chance. If we can give them an exit, they'll take it. The ones who no longer believe will go. We must light the way."

FIFTEEN

The server-bot's red eyes were the last thing Cole remembered. Since then everything else had been hazy. He'd been standing right next to it when the bot ignited. The hair above his left temple was singed clean off. A curl of blackened stubble remained. Duke helped him to his feet and dragged him from the conference room. Cole had been unconscious during the gunfight, and was confused when he saw six dead Crystalline Guards and two of Saba's men looking like Pez-Dispensers.

"Come on Cole, stay with us," Duke said, keeping his arm under Cole's as the team hurried into the freight elevator. Saba brought along her associate, Eliza. An argument was brewing between Duke and Ainsley about going through the tunnels on foot. Ainsley said some of the people needed to rest. Duke warned about getting skewered by the Crystalline Guard. Saba interrupted them and said something that got Cole's attention.

"...above ground, we have another place that should be safe. But there isn't any tunnel that can get us there. We're going to have to risk it. It's about a mile north from here, in Builder's District. Eliza, how are we looking?" Saba asked.

Cole turned to Eliza, his vision swimming to catch up. He saw the redhead pecking viciously at a small glass screen. "The guards are pretty spread out across the city. It was a small patrol that found our station. They'll be alerted when they fail to check-in at the top of the hour, which is in...thirty minutes."

"Terrific, that hardly gives us any time," Saba said, looking at the elevator move through the floors, willing it to speed up.

"We'll make it. We need to stay tight and remain in the shadows," Duke said, reloading his revolver.

"We could spread out and urge the people to leave their homes and storm the gates," Ainsley said.

Saba shook her head. "No one is on the other side yet. It'll take a day or two for the proper journalists we need to reach the outer walls. We need the world watching."

"Here, take Cole," Duke said to Ainsley as they noticed him slipping off the elevator wall. Ainsley grabbed one arm. Saba took the other and held him as he drifted through a painful gray-out.

The elevator shuddered and the horizontal doors opened to the ground floor. Duke stood ready with his revolver and stepped out first. The floor was barren of any life. They exited the warehouse and moved onto a road.

"Where are their cars?" Rafiq asked.

"They were probably on foot patrol, canvassing the area," Eliza answered.

"Well, how'd they find us?" Rafiq asked.

Eliza pointed up to the building they'd left. A tiny slit of light shown from the windows of their office. "They're very good at their jobs. Scanner drones most likely tipped them off."

Rafiq nodded and continued to follow Duke. They walked along the cold center street toward an automated gate. Each of them straddled the steel barrier that raised just three feet from the ground. Ainsley and Saba lifted Cole over the barrier, and then brought up the rear of the group. They stopped at a dividing street corner. Eliza pointed to Sperry Drive, a wide street that led to a bridge which crossed a canal.

The team hustled along the street. Cole's feet were moving but his mind still drawing static. A light fog had crept over the city and it made the Janus Tower glow even brighter, dying the clouds a haunting red.

"Have you ever seen it that color before?" Rafiq asked.

The three women shook their heads.

"What's that sound?" Ainsley asked.

Duke stopped moving and knelt; the group did the same. A deep, almost sub-aural noise shook through the streets like a shockwave. It changed pitch slightly and morphed to a succession of shifting tones. It was as if a canyon had opened up somewhere in the canal, and the great heart of a prehistoric beast was reanimating to life. Hair stood on the nape of Saba's neck.

"Something is powering up. Something big," Saba said. "This city is a creature in and of itself."

"Let's keep moving," Duke advised.

Saba closed her eyes and nodded. "How you doing, Cole?"

Cole was looking at the red laced fog roll about the skyscrapers. All he could hear were thousands of tea-kettles roaring.

They exchanged worried glances and walked on.

Now at the bridge, they had a broader view of the city. The commercial drone traffic had been replaced with scanner drones operated by the Crystalline Guard. The spheres circled the Market Area near Pylône Sept. White spotlight beams cast down through the fog, giving the whole scene a divine look, until the beams shifted to red.

"What's the red beam do?" Rafiq asked.

Eliza glanced up at the sky. "No one knows."

They crossed the bridge and entered Builder's District, a neighborhood of row-houses; relics from a time before Crystalline. There had been modifications: drone portals in every second floor window, solar panels, fog-harvesting nets on every roof to provide recycled water to the neighborhood. Each house had the blinds drawn and the doors sealed. It was mainly used for the building crews that first broke ground on the old city. Now the homes were battery or resource hubs for Crystalline. All of it redirected to main areas of the city. When the power was on, these homes had a continuous hum. Tonight was quiet, except for the heartbeat rumblings from the earth.

Eliza stood by Duke and navigated them through Builder's District via alleyways and cobblestone roads. She explained the next neighborhood, Gaslamp District, was where all the creatives lived, such as artists and musicians. That's where the fallback site was. Kolmogorov Boulevard was the thoroughfare that separated the two districts, and they were a few blocks from it.

Duke looked at Eliza. "So the possibility of a checkpoint or something—"

Eliza nodded.

They walked softly through another impeccably clean alleyway that fed into Kolmogorov Boulevard. That's when Duke saw them. Eight blocks away a collection of Crystalline Guards and white electric-SUVs stood nose to nose in roadblock formation. Eliza showed how the Gaslamp District brushed close to Market District. Duke grinned. They were technically *behind* the roadblock. No one expected people to be moving from a machine-run district. Until the team Duke dealt with failed to check in.

Low blankets of fog rolled along the streets like giant apparitions. Saba said it could provide effective cover as they crossed the boulevard if they could time it right. Duke nodded, but then looked at Cole.

"The poor guy needs to rest," Duke said. "He's concussed."

"We're very close, just six blocks down, one across," Eliza said.

"Alright, take this," Duke said as he handed the revolver to Saba.

"Hey why not—" Rafiq saw Duke's glare and stopped talking.

"You'll need this too just in case." Duke said handing over a small box of extra bullets.

Duke picked up Cole in a fireman's carry position over his shoulder. They waited in a crouched position on the edge of the boulevard, waiting for the fog to roll in. The Crystalline Guard's backs all turned to them. A few minutes passed, and that's when a huge gray swathe barreled through, partly illuminated by the electric-SUVs.

They took their chance and ran.

The group bolted across the boulevard. Rafiq did a wide stride sprint across and watched Eliza, Ainsley and Saba trail close behind. Duke hustled along the best he could, but wanted to be careful with Cole. Although Duke would never admit this, his legs were killing him from earlier. He was convinced he sprained his ankle during the firefight in the conference room. Wincing along, he was nearly halfway across when he saw a light beam cast from an alleyway in the Gaslamp District, but couldn't be sure because of the thick fog.

Finally Duke made it across when Cole began to retch. His wails echoed through the streets. Duke grabbed his mouth and looked at Eliza. "How far?"

"This way, we'll need—" Eliza looked ahead and went ghost white.

A flashlight beam bounced from an alley, then another, and another. If they double-backed they'd be back on the boulevard. Saba stepped ahead of everyone and crouched with the shaking revolver pointed at the beams of light. Sweat was leaking from her forehead. She focused on her breathing and soon her hand steadied.

Now they could hear footsteps. They were close, no more than fifty yards. Then, as quickly as the lights appeared, they were gone. That mechanical shuddering bore from the city once more, adding to the horror Saba felt. *They know we're here,* she thought, gripping revolver's wooden handle.

"Building 13A, routine sweep," said a voice from the alley where there was once light. Saba crept to the edge of the alley and peered into it.

A faraway voice responded into the radio. "Copy Echo-team, confirmed Building 13A, you may proceed." A buzzing sound from an unlocking mechanical door rang and the guards entered the apartment complex. Soon the lights were gone.

Saba breathed out a long sigh, thanking God. "C'mon, nearly there,"

They navigated through the Gaslamp District as the sounds of the city grew louder. Between the lull of the city sounds you could hear Cole's moaning, his concussion getting worse. They paused for a moment to review the map when Cole retched again. This time someone heard it.

"That one of our guys?" said a guard from inside a closed café. Two guards exited the café just feet from Saba. They rounded the corner and saw a peculiar sight: six people flush against the wall, and a giant carrying an unconscious man. The silver barrel shimmered in the residual moonlight and soon flashed bright white. The explosion from the revolver drummed through the silent city streets. One of the guards fell back with remnants of his thigh in pieces. Saba fired off seven more shots, at close range, until the weak metal clicking of the revolver cap sounded. The guard who wasn't shot stood frozen until he realized the hand cannon was empty. He reached for his radio. "Atlas Alarm," was all he could say before Saba tackled him, striking him the face with the smoking barrel.

The next twenty seconds were remarkable. Streetlights powered on as if someone flicked a switch to a large auditorium. The droning sound beneath the city grew louder and the sidewalk began to vibrate. Duke thought about doubling back to the Utility District when he watched Kolmogorov Boulevard open like a new fault line. The streets folded beneath the sidewalk in an accordion-like fashion, and cobalt walls ascended from below. The wall grew a foot, then another, and soon it reached ten feet high, then twenty.

"They're cordoning off the city. Eliza, talk to me," Saba said, trying to catch her breath.

"Four blocks north," Eliza said.

The group ran by the closed café as alarms sounded throughout the city; more streetlights were coming to life and the distant sound of scanner drones could be heard amongst the chaos. They turned down an alley, one Saba and Ainsley had been down many times before, only to find a cobalt wall rising flush between the two neighboring buildings. The space between could barely fit an envelope through.

"This way," Eliza pointed as she rerouted her map. They scaled the mechanical dumpsters and hopped over a chain-link fence into a chute used mainly for drainage. It spit them out onto an adjacent street. Continuing north, in the direction of the apartment complex, they saw search lights to the south of them. Duke struggled to keep up, he felt like Cole was somehow getting heavier. Ainsley tried assisting Duke, but he told her to keep moving. A scanner drone flew over them and banked high amongst the buildings, its spotlight brushing over them for a moment.

They paused at the corner of Morse Street and 3rd Avenue and caught their breath; Duke trailing behind. Eliza spoke in between gasps. "At the end of the block is the apartment." She took two breaths. "It's the silver townhouse." The ground beneath them began to rumble again.

"Can't stop now guys," Saba said, leading the way down the newly lit street. That's when everything changed. Morse Street began to shudder and open between Saba and her team. "C'mon, c'mon!" Saba shouted. Rafiq and Eliza leapt over the chasm. Ainsley followed and jumped on top of the wall as it rose. She leapt off and looked back at Duke, all the veins in his neck pulsing, like a thoroughbred on the final straightaway at the Kentucky Derby. The wall was now five feet and rising fast. He tossed Cole on the top like a lifeguard tossing a drowning victim from a pool; but Cole fell back onto Duke. "No." Saba's voice faded over the rising wall.

A drumming of footsteps came from behind Duke. He saw the spotlights and laser scopes, then the men who carried the equipment. The Praetorian Guards. They looked almost robotic. Moving in quick and even patterns they filled the streets and leveled their lights and scopes on Duke and the unconscious Cole. Duke knew there was no play here. He dropped to his knees and put his hands behind his head. Seconds later he was surrounded by men his size, dressed in all black, with glowing headsets and rifles he'd never seen before. Their black masks made them faceless, like a personification of evil only seen in nightmares.

The rifles were trained on Duke while two men zip-tied Cole's hands and feet together. One of the men swung his rifle behind his back, reached into his pocket and took out what looked to be a small salt packet. Another man held Duke's face. He tore the paper pack underneath Duke's nose. The scent, Duke thought, was a bubblegum flavor, similar to what he had as a kid at little league baseball. As soon as that image of him as a first-baseman appeared, his vision blurred and tunneled to the point of total blackness. A moment later he lay unconscious on the ground.

Duke did not see the electric-SUVs pull up. He did not feel himself being loaded into the trucks and driven away beside Cole. Saba, Ainsley, Rafiq and Eliza weren't aware either. They simply saw the walls rising into the night sky. They had no choice but to sojourn on to their last place of refuge, hoping that hadn't been found. Blocks away, the buildings surrounding Janus Tower began to power on again, the drone traffic resumed, and Crystalline charged back to life.

SIXTEEN

Cole stirred awake to the birdsong of snow quails, a sound he hadn't heard since childhood. *A dream.* He turned over in bed and pulled the quilt underneath his chin. It wasn't a soft quilt; the bristles were too harsh to ever snuggle with entirely. Usually it required a buffer: sheets or another blanket. The only quilt Cole remembered with this much bristle was in his parent's home back in Colorado. He pulled the quilt closer. It felt like a wino with three-day old stubble was cuddling next to him. Cole shuddered and pushed the quilt away. The last thing he saw was a plastic statue in faux-gold holding a batting stance. *STATE CHAMPS,* the plaque read. Cheers of the Timberwolves High School students sounded from far away canyons of his mind.

"Full count, man on second—" Cole muttered and kicked the quilt off of him. Pins and needles surged up the nape of his neck to his head. Above him was a poster of Marisa Miller with an iPod set in the place her bikini bottom should be. Cole grinned and then panicked. He was in his boyhood room, back in Longmont, Colorado. "What the hell?" he said, slamming his eyes shut then opening again wide, in hopes it would change his surroundings. It didn't.

The door opened and a woman with bobbed blonde hair with curled ends entered. Her hair looked like a yellow cloud following a weathered face. "Sweetheart," she whispered.

"Mom?" Cole said, sitting up in bed.

"Easy, easy," she said, picking up the bristly quilt and laying it back on his legs. "You've been through hell, Colton. You need to rest."

"Am I home?"

"Yes. Your father and I picked you up from the hospital three days ago. He was able to fly his Cessna. The doctors said you were fine to fly, thank god. It would've been torture to have you stuck in the car for that long."

"Duke…what about—"

"Paid medical leave. The benefits of a union job." Her mouth grew to a small smile. "Your friend Ra*fick* sent over an Edible Arrangement. He's a very sweet man. By tomorrow I think you'll be able to stomach sweets."

"No...where's Ainsley?"

Cole's mother sighed. "I sent her an email, but you know how she is. That darn city is all she cares about. Maybe we'll hear back."

"No, I was with her. She's in trouble."

Cole's mother leaned back suspiciously and then was reminded of the head trauma the doctors said he had sustained. "Don't you worry Cole, you're just confused. I'll bring you—"

The door burst open and Cole saw the quick flashes of a golden retriever's tail set high, wagging fiercely. Two giant paws stuck to the quilt and Cole's mother laughed. "C'mon Sally, giddy-up there," she said. Cole felt the bedside depress and then a golden retriever leaped onto his lap. Sally licked Cole's face and chin and face again; stepped on his crotch twice and then nestled beside Cole's thigh. Sally smelt of fresh cut grass and wet dog.

What's happening to me? Cole went to argue but felt overwhelmed with fatigue. He lay back with his hand on a panting retriever. His mom smiled as she left the room.

* * *

When Cole woke up again Sally was gone. For a split second he saw no room at all, only the mere outlines of a phantom enclosure traced with black lines against a white plain. He blinked and saw the baseball trophy, the look of lust in Marisa Miller's eyes, and a burning sun set behind the black and gray Rockies. It seemed the window was a video screen with residual static, but really it was a light dusting of snow falling through a windless night.

Cole felt remarkable. He was able to push the bristle quilt, covers, and sheets off of him and stand without wincing. The pain had dampened from sharp to dull. Cole pulled on a pair of Levi's that were folded beside an MIT sweatshirt, folded neatly in the way a mother only knows how to do. His father was in the Air Force and folded too efficiently, like he used a ruler on each edge.

Now clothed and warm, Cole made his way down the stairs and was welcomed by the briny smell of chicken noodle soup. A fire crackled in the den and he saw the wool-socked feet of his father, Rex, who was sunk deep into a recliner. Sally blocked Cole at the end of the steps and barked happily, dancing around him. Cole heard the familiar squeak and yaw of the recliner as his father climbed out of it. He tossed a Clive Cussler paperback on the coffee table. Rex, despite being in his seventies, still had the squat but fit look of a fighter pilot. Rex brushed crumbs off his white goatee and hugged his son. Cole stood with his arms at his sides in the embrace and then, as if by Pavlovian affection, wrapped his arms around his father and wept.

"Glad you're back, boy," Rex said.

They held the embrace for a long time. Cole could smell the Barbasol and Pinaud Clubman on his father. He remembered how the scent would always steam out of the bathrooms during the weekdays.

"Dad, what happened?"

"Sit down, sit down," Rex said, showing his son to the yellow-jacket plaid couch that lay beside the recliner. Cole sank into the old cushions as Rex tossed another pine log into the fire. Above the mantle was an oil painting of the family: Cole, Ainsley, Rex, and Margret, Sally too.

Margret came out of the kitchen holding a wooden tray with a crimson bowl of steaming chicken noodle soup. She walked carefully, moving like she was balancing a glass of nitroglycerin, but with efficient confidence, not spilling a drop. "Here you go, sweetheart."

"Thanks, mom," Cole said, slurping a silver spoon of the soup. He smiled for the first time since arriving in Colorado. His mom always made the best chicken noodle soup; it had to be the extra thyme and garlic rice she added. "Delicious," he said.

Cole's parents looked at him with both of their heads titled slightly to the right and smiled at the same time, like aliens. Cole shuddered, but the warmth of the soup felt like an invisible blanket wrapping around his soul. Margret sat in an adjacent wicker chair with her hands in her lap.

Rex sipped his vodka and ice, pursed his lips and looked at his son. "There was a gas leak in your building, Cole. You tried to get out but fell down the stairs. It was by the grace of God," Margret made the sign of the cross, "that a neighbor found you. The doctors said you sustained a severe concussion and experienced mild gas exposure. Confusion, headaches, weakness, et cetera. As Captain Driggs would've said, 'your body was FUBAR'ed.'" Rex mustered a grin. "Your boss, Duke, was the one who called us. The doctors said you were good to fly, so I gassed up the Skyhawk and made my way over. I wish I had access to the F-18s still, would've been there in a quarter of the time. Anyway, I'm glad you're okay, son."

Cole nodded, trying to process the last few days. He remembered coming home for dinner after a long day of work. Rafiq was annoying but that was a commonality, so it didn't stand out as an isolating detail. He remembered showering and then reheating leftovers, another common detail. Then sleeping and having a troubling nightmare. The next memory was the ptarmigans arguing away in the Colorado high grass this morning. Cole slurped some more soup and sat back in the warmth.

"Do we have any beer?" Cole asked as he pushed away the empty bowl.

Margret nervously looked at Rex, who was smiling. "Relax Margret, it's man's oldest remedy," Rex said, getting up. A moment later he was back with a tall brown bottle. "Some kid down the block started up his own micro-brewery. He made me switch my lifelong affiliation with Coors." Rex handed his son the bottle.

Cole took a long gulp and the hops bounced bitterly to the back of his tongue and blended well with the aftertaste of the soup. A mellow buzz soon set in, reminding Cole of the high altitude the town sat at. Rex turned on the Packers game and they watched in comfortable silence. A John Denver song played from the kitchen as his mom washed up. Cole sat back and smiled. The folk singer was right, it sure did feel good to be back home again.

SEVENTEEN

There are plenty of ways to wake up in the morning happy. For some it's a coffee maker that's synchronized with their alarm clock. It could be having their kids asking for a pancake breakfast. For Duke though, it was waking up beside Cassandra. She was Duke's fiancé for a few months until one day he came home to find the ring on his kitchen table. That loss turned his heart into stone. That is until his future wife came along years later. Nevertheless, Duke didn't want to admit it, but he knew it was for the best. Duke and Cassandra were like two unstable atoms. They both were competitive, passionate and craved one another. However the compatibility, just going through the minutiae of life, didn't work for either of them. The day she left, Duke went to his first Alcoholics Anonymous meeting and had gone every day since for years.

When Duke woke up, he had a tremendous headache, like he had been chewing on rocks all night. He rolled away from the morning light and felt his arm brush against something warm. A woman with straight brown hair and porcelain skin lay beside him. Duke reeled; believing it to be a dream, he set his large hand on the small of her back. The warmth radiated against his calloused palms.

"Cassandra?"

The woman rolled over and flashed those unforgettable piercing green eyes, like cat eyes, and smiled. "Morning, sunshine," she said.

"What the hell is this?"

"You got pretty wild last night." Cassandra cleared her throat. "I can't believe Higgins kept on serving us."

The headache of a violent hangover enhanced Duke's confusion. The pain kept escalating, endlessly, like a Shepard Tone. Duke moaned, burying his head into the pillows. Sobriety, the ever fragile chain, had been broken. Loathing crept alongside the headache like a close friend. Duke lay there for a few minutes in silence until he heard Cassandra rustling through the sheets. She climbed out of bed and walked to the window to pour herself water from a craft. All she wore was black lace boy shorts. Duke watched her. Hating her, hating himself for succumbing to his own weakness. *Last night…* Duke couldn't remember. The last thing he could recall was leaving work after the damn pipe exploded. Everything after that was whiskey laden, *or is that a false memory?* Not uncommon to professional drinkers, even the retired ones.

Cassandra walked slowly, sensually back toward the bed and tickled Duke's feet that peeked from beneath the blankets. Then she burrowed under the sheets and covers between his legs and climbed up his calves, then thighs, and suddenly, as if by miracle, his headache and loathing faded. Duke looked below the sheets and she smiled back at him. He threw his head back and tried to enjoy the moment. His heart thundered rhythmically in a powerful beat. Duke wanted to keep this feeling forever; a frivolous pursuit, like grasping dandelion seeds in the wind. They made love the rest of the morning. By the time Duke's grandfather clock chimed noon they were famished. They washed up, dressed, and went to the diner across the street.

"Is this how marathon runners feel?" Cassandra asked as she picked up a handful of sweet potato fries and dunked them in ketchup.

Duke looked at her. "Satiated?"

Cassandra gave the grin of a vixen. "Starving, exhausted…exhilarated."

Duke shrugged and picked up a juicy cheeseburger the size of two hockey pucks stacked together, sautéed onions wedged between. "I guess so," he said taking a wide bite into the burger, which spread ketchup across his cheeks. He snagged a few fries from the basket and washed it down with a light beer. *One light beer will be fine.* Cassandra smiled at him with those green cat eyes.

Today I'll have fun, tomorrow I'll get back on the wagon. I'll call my sponsor. Tomorrow, yeah, tomorrow.

The only floors of the Janus Tower without windows were floor five, eighteen, and seventy-two. The first two were ventilation for the server rooms and other building utilities. The seventy-second floor was designated as an entertainment and design ideation lab. Designers who studied in Berlin and Tokyo were the first to arrive, then Hollywood innovators became involved. The teams on "Seventy-two" as it was referred to by other employees were bound by nondisclosure agreements and non-competes for life. Rumors and speculation from other Janus employees flurried around the cafés about what happened up there.

Inside the labs of floor seventy-two, a flurry of engineers were busy tending to the cascading code in front of their terminals. Thin smoke trails rose from technician desks as they worked soldering irons on circuit boards that lay embedded into what looked like a wetsuit. Leif, a senior technician, set down his soldering iron, pushed away his magnifying eyeglasses and replaced them with his regular wide frame glasses, giving him a stark resemblance to Buddy Holly. Removing the static bracelet, gloves, hairnet and apron, he exited the lab and walked down the lucite hallways which mimicked the time and season with ambient light patterns. An amber and purple hue stretched down the long hallway. *Sunset.* Leif checked his watch. He was off by a couple of minutes. It was technically dusk now.

Leif entered floor seventy-two's private breakroom, which housed his most prized creation: Barista-bot. Behind a eucalyptus counter was a silver cylinder which had several arms and hoses attached to it. Someone put a Folger's baseball cap on the cylinder's top. Leif shook his head and removed the hat. He'd drink sulfuric acid before touching that brand of coffee.

"Good evening, Amanda," Leif said.

Lights along the cylinder's base and middle lit up, some yellows, mostly greens. The hose shivered back like a spine. *Glug-glug-glug-glug*, followed by sibilant spats as the arms stretched in an off-rhythm clunking. The cylinder settled down and turned slightly toward Leif.

"Hello, Leif, it is a nice evening. The usual?"

"Yes, thanks Amanda,"

"Don't… mention it."

The robot went to work, its various arms moving about like a dancing Vishnu. Pale coffee beans slid from a tube and into a roasting pan. Leif smiled at his creation and grabbed a banana from a glass bowl and began to peel it. Taking a penknife from his back pocket, Leif meticulously sliced the banana into perfect five centimeter discs. He then dropped a dollop of honey on each top and garnished with cinnamon.

The TV was on in the corner of the room. It was covering the latest results of the Crystalline Obstacle Course Race. A hellish feat of endurance and strength. The mayor of Crystalline seemed to be there, along with other members of the societal government. The mayor gave a short apology about the sudden power outage two days ago, stating that the city's servers were receiving regular maintenance when they uncovered a few unforeseen problems. The only thing they could do was shut the power down to prevent further damage to the servers. Leif heard whispers of some video being shown right before then. A woman calling for rebellion. It sounded far-fetched. He knew it was just the imagination of his colleagues. Still though, it made him uncomfortable. *Why would anyone want to rebel?* This city had provided an environment for Leif to thrive: intellectually, physically, sexually. Forget Silicon Valley, this was Valhalla for geniuses.

"Leif, I have your white mocha latte," Amanda said. A thin metal arm carefully placed a ceramic mug on the counter. The foam design in the milk and coffee was of a square rigger ship, three masts, and it seemed an anchor was in the process of striking the coffee seas.

"Thank you, Amanda," Leif said, taking his coffee. He walked back to the lab and figured he'd check on Martin and his latest project. Leif punched in a key code to a glass screen. The airlocks unlatched and the door slid open. Through another set of doors, Leif saw Martin looking through a large two-way mirror. Beyond the mirror lay two men on hospital beds. They were both clad in haptic feedback suits, which looked similar to wetsuits. Various wires and hoses stuck out of the back of the suits and ran along the bed. Intravenous lines, catheters, and sensors connected to the various ports in the ground. They wore neural-synch skull caps and VR goggles. The massive man, who had a wrist tag that read DUKE, was shuddering, as if he were suffering from some deep nightmare.

Martin was rubbing Vaseline on the sore marks that wrapped his cheeks when he noticed Leif drinking one his ridiculous lattes. "Hi, Leif," Martin said.

"Evening, sir. Everything running smoothly?" Leif asked. He walked over to the monitors and checked both of the men's vitals.

Martin nodded and grimaced. "So far, so good."

Duke shuddered again in the bed. His jaw and fists clenched tight, then released.

"What's the deal with the big guy?" Leif asked with a tinge of nervousness.

Martin smiled. "He didn't have a Janus profile, so I scanned the servers for his photo and came across this woman named Cassandra, a nymphomaniac cokehead he nearly married. Somehow *she* left *him*. Stranger than fiction, my friend."

"You re-animated her into his life?" Leif asked.

Martin nodded.

Leif considered warning him about the neurological implications of virtually reincarnating old relationships, but let that moment pass. Martin outranked Leif tenfold, and he learned to never to question the men and women who gave him unlimited resources for any idea he had. *Don't bite the hand…*

"Do you need my help with bringing them back?" Leif asked.

"In time…but I don't think that'll be for awhile."

Leif's eyes widened. "Sir, it's been forty-eight hours already."

Martin looked at Leif with his stone gray eyes. Leif's Adam's apple bobbled and he sipped his coffee to give him a minute of composure.

"Never mind," Leif said.

Martin put his hands behind his back and turned toward the two hospital beds and grinned like a wolf seeing wounded prey fall along a prairie. When Leif left the room he could've sworn he heard Martin laughing through the doors.

EIGHTEEN

Ainsley Wainwright had been on the treadmill for nearly an hour, clocking in just over eight miles. Anytime she felt stressed, her body screamed for it to move and sweat. Saba had tried teaching her yoga, but found Ainsley would get impatient. Ainsley said running was a moving meditation for her. She could feel the anxiety seep out of her. Today though, the sweat poured out by the gallon and she couldn't shake the desperate loathing. She was responsible for leading her brother to this city. Now he was paying the price. Shaking her head, she cranked up the speed on the treadmill and boosted the volume on her headphones. Tupac's "2 of Amerikaz Most Wanted" blared out. Ainsley sprinted until her thighs began to burn and fill with imagined cement, spreading, paralyzing; a sharp pain dug right under her ribs, all the body's alarm bells ringing. After another mile she hit the big yellow button which shifted the treadmill into a subdued "cool down" mode. "No More Pain" came on next. She smirked at its irony. That's when Saba entered the room holding smoothies.

Ainsley pulled out her headphones. "Any news?"

Saba looked at Ainsley, then at the floor, shaking her head.

"Dammit." Ainsley chucked her headphones at the window. They bounced off the glass and fell to the ground.

"We'll find them. I have my feelers out. But I need help. Have you connected with that Zeina girl?"

Ainsley hopped off the treadmill and wiped her face with a towel. "Zelda," Ainsley said, taking a Crystalline smoothie from Saba's hand. "No, she's a ghost. I called her café and there hasn't been an answer."

Saba sat in a wingback chair and looked out the window at the green lines of drone traffic and sipped her smoothie. "We also have to stay focused on the tasks at hand. I've had some of the journalists respond; getting them here will be the next challenge. Some of them want us to foot the bill."

Ainsley grunted. "Terrific." She sipped the delicious strawberry, banana and peanut butter smoothie. "What are we going to show them? The sealed gates? We had our chance and it failed. We need to find Cole and Duke and then reassess."

Saba went to argue, but bit her tongue. She didn't want to tell Ainsley that the odds of seeing her brother again were very low. Saba heard rumors of a reprogramming prison. A system that can convince its enemies to love and eventually work for Janus. That way they never go missing in the eyes of the Federal government. The new Crystalleans still file their taxes and live a prosperous life; the memories of rebellion fade into the ether. Saba reminded herself they were only rumors, but it sounded probable. The scientists and programmers that worked for Janus were the best in the world.

"There is the other option," Saba said, crossing her legs.

Ainsley took a seat near Saba and began stretching. "Lemme guess. Rafiq spoke to you?"

Saba nodded. "The man's got a point. With his knowledge of the tunnels and Eliza's mapping ability, I'm sure we can find a way out of the city. It can be a way to talk to the journalists."

"And leave Cole and Duke? Leave them locked up?" Ainsley stood and began stretching her arms to the floor. She came up from the stretch with a look of despair. "Just leave them?"

"If we can get Crystalline to fall—"

"Ah, what does that even mean anymore? They're too big to fail. They're a multi-trillion dollar company. How can something that massive ever die? It'll be like trying to kill a planet or a star."

"Well, we're already killing this planet—"

"You know what I mean. This is impossible."

"Invincibility lies in the defense; the possibility of victory in the attack."

"Oh shut the hell up, Sun Tzu," Ainsley said, looking out the window at the neon skyline.

"You know I'm right, Ains. The Janus Corporation can be taken down. It happened to Face—"

The door opened and Rafiq stepped in with Eliza, who was holding a glass tablet computer. "I think we have something," Rafiq said eagerly.

"And?" Saba said.

Eliza stepped forward with the glass tablet now facing Ainsley and Saba. "When the walls began rising inside Crystalline it meant those areas of the city had power on entirely. Some of it activated the electricity in nearby buildings, which turned security cameras back on. I was able to patch into a storefront's camera that was on the block Cole and Duke were when the walls began to rise. We caught still images of them being… captured by the Praetorian Guards," Eliza said. She swiped on the screen and it showed grainy images of Duke surrendering and a few guards holding something beneath his nose; immediately he went limp and fell beside Cole. A red electric-SUV reversed up to the two unconscious bodies and loaded them into the back.

"Jesus Christ," Ainsley said, looking away from the screen.

"I was able to find footage of the same red electric-SUV pulling into the Janus Tower," Eliza said.

A silence lingered for a moment.

"I'm sorry, Ainsley. We need to discuss plan B. We can't help them if they're in the tower," Saba said.

Ainsley stared at the window for a long time, saying nothing. She'd gone numb. Ainsley knew Saba was right. They had no more support. Cole and Duke were locked in a fortified tower. There was only one hand left to play, and it involved fleeing the city. Ainsley walked onto the balcony and stared at the sinking sun, dying the mountains blue and gold, willing herself to find another plan. But she kept drawing blanks.

NINETEEN

A bender stops being fun when the drugs run out and the bar goes dry. That's when the body begins to wake up and realize the horrible damage it sustained. Some musicians from the 1970s and 1980s were able to keep their benders going for as long as three days. The cocaine and whiskey seemed to flow from an endless tap. If they didn't die when the tap shut off, the incredible hangover would begin. A bender of that magnitude can take a week or more to recover from. Duke was on day two of recovery after a four-day-long binge.

He lay in bed beside empty whiskey bottles and powdery mirrors. Two other women had been with him last night, but wandered off like roaming coyotes. The apartment was destroyed. Someone left the blender on all night. It had shorted out and caught fire just before dawn. It cooked half of the refrigerator and an original photo from Anne Geddes. Duke, who once was a competitive hammer thrower, found the hammer weight in his closet on the first night, just as the second delivery of cocaine arrived. The hammer weight went through his living room wall and into the bathroom. It broke the wrist of a vagrant who had followed them back from the bar for free drugs. The vagrant went onto the balcony holding his limp wrist, trying to compose himself. Duke could've sworn a person stumble off the balcony and fall eleven stories. But he never heard sirens, so Duke assumed it was a hallucination.

Cassandra had slept with three men who weren't Duke during this four-day weekend. It didn't matter. Duke had bedded five women and potentially a man during this period. Two dogs had straggled into the apartment and mated too. A cat strayed into the room as well. The front doorknob had been destroyed, making it sway with the wind. But the cat soon wised up to the situation and scamper off.

Duke leaned off the putrid mattress and vomited into a potted plant, then rolled over moaning. '*Tomorrow*,' *you fucking idiot*. Duke needed air. He needed to leave the apartment. He couldn't bear to look at the shameful evidence of his addiction. He pulled on a pair of whiskey-stained jeans and a linen button-down, also stained, but with blood. Cassandra was passed out on the couch in the living room beside a dog. Duke cleaned off a dusty coke mirror and held it under her face for a moment; when he saw it steam up he nodded to himself and left.

The elevator was stuck on his floor, its doors stuck open. A walking cane with a brass eagle head was jammed into one of the doors. Sparks coughed from the control panel. Duke glanced at his bloody knuckles and nodded, shamefully remembering that detail. He took the stairs. After the first set of stairs his vision began to list. Duke grabbed hold of the railing and collected himself. "You got this. Get outside, it'll be fine," Duke slurred to himself. He descended the steps again. The next flight was blurry, but okay. The last flight, from the second to the first floor, Duke blacked out and fell down a set of ten concrete stairs. The cartilage in his nose became sand and his femur broke in two places. Duke's right humerus bone jutted through the skin beyond his elbow, collecting dust.

The fall would've killed a frailer man, but lucky for Duke he was built like an ox.

Inside the real world of floor seventy-two, Duke lay on his hospital bed panting. The fall, while virtual, was real to the brain. When he fell down the staircase Duke shuddered violently, shaking loose some of the sensors in his neural-synch skull cap. The sensors were now askew. It was just enough for the fidelity of the virtual world Duke occupied to tear at the seams. Leif didn't notice, as he was tending to a problem with Amanda the barista-bot. She hadn't successfully determined the differences in almond and soy milk.

While Duke lay at the bottom of the virtual staircase in agonizing pain he saw something out of the corner of his eye. It was another hand, *his* hand in a hospital bed. The scrim of his reality was tearing into the real world. *Whathafuck?* Duke spread his fingers out and saw the fingers in the hospital bed move. *Whathafuck?* He continued to peer through the scrim and saw it was some sort of hospital or lab. The severity of his injuries caused his vision to blacken. *No no no no.* And the lights went out.

Cassandra found him hours later. She called the paramedics. It took a four-man team to lift Duke into the ambulance. He had several surgeries to reset his arm and fix his leg. By nightfall, Duke lay in a hospital bed tucked under blue sheets. Sometime around dusk he woke up and glanced at his right hand. In the virtual world it lay on blue sheets with blood stained knuckles. In reality, he could see his real hand on white sheets. *Whathafuck?* Duke shifted his weight to shake away the strange mirror image. He imagined it was a side effect from the copious amounts of drugs he'd consumed over the last four days. Duke began to weep. He'd truly lost his mind. The more he shook, the more the scrim opened. He wailed and screamed and shuddered. More and more the scrim opened. He could see his feet, and the far end of the hospital bed. *Whathafuck? Whathafuck?!* He wiggled his toes and saw both of them, the virtual and the real, like mirrors against each other moving with a slight delay.

It took him another twelve hours, in between morphine-induced naps, to orient himself with the real world via the virtual one. Duke moved his right hand and felt underneath the hospital bed a series of wires. He tugged on them and for a split second the scrim vanished. Only slight outlines of the virtual world remained. He saw Cole lying beside him. The pain was remarkable. Releasing the wires brought back the virtual world in a disturbing flash. "*WHATHAFUCK?!*" Duke cried out, which echoed in both worlds.

Soon he saw an overweight nurse come in and check his vitals. Through the scrim opening he saw a man, holding a ceramic coffee mug, with eyes wide. He set down his mug with care and leaned against Duke's body. The man seemed to be adjusting something on Duke's head, but he couldn't see. Then, as quick as a thunder bolt, the virtual world filled in the scrim opening and Duke was re-immersed. He leaned over his bedside and mewled, pressing the IV button, warm morphine pumping through his veins. Duke felt the high creep its way into his body like a friendly snake. He lay there immobile and wept.

TWENTY

"No, I said a three-quarter inch socket. This is three-sixteenth," said Rex from underneath the 1951 Chevy Pickup.

Cole rifled through the red toolbox. Sally, the golden retriever, was trying to catch a bee out on the driveway. "Dad, you really need to organize this thing. It's a mess."

"That was *my* father's toolbox, and I'm leaving it how he had it. This is how I remember him."

A small grin moved across Cole's face. He couldn't argue with that. Everything else in the garage was immaculate and organized. White pegboards lined the walls above a black workstation. Tools were delineated by size from left to right. Slip-joint pliers, needle-nose pliers, linemen pliers; the wall was complete with everything a former fighter pilot and car enthusiast needed. Rex Wainwright was molded by the Air Force Academy and even in retirement he upheld their values with pride. With the exception of the nostalgic red toolbox.

"Found it," Cole said, dropping the socket into a dirty hand that emerged from beneath the pickup truck.

"Alright, let's see here," Rex said. The cracking sound of the socket wrench could be heard over Sally's barking. She saw a squirrel and wanted everyone to know. Then a pattering sound of oil striking the pan echoed as Rex rolled out from under the truck. Cole handed his father a rag and he wiped his hands. "Now we wait until she's empty."

"I know dad, I've done this before."

"Well sometimes a process bears repeating. That's how things remain consistent. Decreases the chances for error."

Cole nodded. He had heard the same lecture countless times growing up. Cole sauntered over to Sally and pet her. She looked up and gave a goofy smile the way dogs do. He smiled at her and threw a stick across the front lawn.

Sally went into a hot pursuit. Cole stretched in the morning light and realized he hadn't felt this good in a long time. The concussion symptoms were gone. The Union gave Cole two months off with pay. There was no point rushing back to his apartment. Life was good here. His mother's cooking was exceptional, and the Colorado air seemed to speed up the healing process. Despite the strange nightmare he'd had last night—he could've sworn it was Duke in his shouting—he was feeling great. He watched Sally bring the slobbery stick back to his feet. Cole chucked it further. Sally took off and Cole laughed. He was happy.

Rex came out of the garage holding a wrench that had the mouth of an angler fish. "You want to take the oil filter off, or should I do all the work?" Rex asked. Cole took the wrench and headed back to the garage. The morning light shifted from its golden blue to plainer white daylight. The glare reflected off the chrome bumper of the pickup truck. Cole shielded his eyes from the sharp reflection and in that instant he could've sworn he saw the traced outline of the Chevy and the entire garage. Everything was against a white plain, black lines sketched out the pegboard wall of tools, the workstation, the family pickup truck, the framed photos, the garage door string with the tennis ball attached to the end; then it flashed and reanimated to life. Cole shook his head with a furrowed brow. *Damn concussion.* He drank some water and got to work on the engine.

* * *

"We can cut along conduit eighty-seven, and if the doors aren't sealed we can get back on the hyperloop tunnel that took you in here," Eliza said, pointing at her glass tablet screen.

"And if it *is* sealed shut?" Rafiq asked.

"We'll double back and push to conduit ninety-one, though there might be guards there because we'd be getting close to an active tunnel."

Rafiq scratched the black stubble on his chin. "Makes sense. Once we're out we can regroup and connect with the journalists."

Saba stood above them with her arms crossed. "We have twenty confirmed. I've paid for their flights. For now I told them to meet at the Francis Court Hotel."

"Better than nothing," Rafiq said.

"I wish there were more," Saba said. "Your friend Zelda is still a ghost, but I'd like to find her when we're over there. Can you hook that up?"

"I'll try. I mean, we'll be exiting through her café, so I'm sure she'll be there," Rafiq said. "How's Ainsley holding up?"

"I should be asking you. You're leaving your friends?"

Rafiq shrugged. "Like you said, this is our only move. Plus I wanna get out of here," Rafiq said, downing his head in shame.

Saba nodded. "Ainsley's upset. But she understands."

Ainsley came out of the bathroom. Though her eyes were red from crying, she held her chin up and shoulders back. She'd accepted the fate and was submitting to Saba's plan on faith. "Ready?"

Eliza wrapped up the charging port for her gear and stuffed it into a messenger bag. "One moment," Eliza said, walking over to the kitchen counter where a coffee machine burped. She poured herself a tall cup of warm coffee in a Crystalline CrossFit thermos and sealed it shut. She wiped the finger prints off of the craft and nodded at Saba. "That's the last of the fingerprints in this place. I don't think they'll find it for a long time anyway, but better to be safe."

Saba loaded up her backpack, and then checked Duke's revolver. "Take a last look at that skyline. It'll be a long time until we see it again from the inside," Saba said.

The team took a moment and watched the buzzing lines of drone traffic against the nighttime neon hues. It was a clear night, and the moon was waning to a small white sliver in the sky. Ainsley looked out at Janus Tower and restrained herself from putting her hand against the window. "Hang in there guys," she said as a single tear rolled down her face and dropped to the carpet.

A couple minutes later, the team left the building via a service elevator. They moved quick and close in the night, like a pack of jackals. Through a manhole cover they made their way to conduit eighty-seven. The doors weren't sealed, just locked, which took the better part of a half-hour to break through. Once they managed to bypass the door, the team started their escape from Crystalline.

TWENTY ONE

Duke's hatred for hospitals started at six years old. It was at the bedside of his dying mother where the misery overwhelmed him. In her final moments, Duke watched her gasping for air, for life, and her neck, riddled with tumors, convulsed like a dozen Adam's Apples. Stern-faced doctors and nurses moved in and out with the carelessness of commuters breezing through a train station. The entire scene was dreadful, but it was the smell Duke could never get used to. The sterility was the same in hospitals; it wasn't bleach, but something cleaner. When Duke was young he thought the cleaners were meant to mask the smell of death. The putrid and organic scent of decay covered by layers of cleaning chemicals. Duke never had children, which gave him relief, because he loathed the day his kin would be born in a hospital. New life starting amongst the scent of death. *Cradle and grave in the same damn building.*

Cassandra watched Duke shudder in his sleep. She frowned, knowing his deep hatred for places like this. She hoped today he'd be discharged. It had been two weeks in the virtual world, when in reality it was much shorter. Duke emptied his morphine drip every day. Cassandra looked at the empty intravenous bag with envy, like a hungry lioness who came upon the bones of a kill. Duke whimpered, tossing his head back and forth.

He wasn't dreaming. The virtual world could only go so deep. Reconstructing dreams were only at a rudimentary level. Janus had yet to perfect it. For Duke it was nearly suffering in a void until he awoke again.

Cassandra was reading a copy of *Cosmopolitan* when Duke's steely eyes flashed opened. "Water," he grunted. Cassandra jumped at the sound of his voice. She hustled to untangle from the pretzel-like position she'd been lying in for the last few hours. Pouring water from a plastic craft into a paper cup, she handed it to Duke. Sweat beaded along his brow and upper lip. His leg was in traction, splinted straight to let the femur and hip mend. The compound fracture was being healed from a full-length cast on his left arm.

A meek nurse entered the room with a red folder. He watched her carefully. The nurse checked the vitals and replaced the saline bag. Duke grunted, "When will I get the hell out of here?"

The tired nurse, who wavered from apathetic to irritated, gave a curt response. "You're going to be here for at least another week."

Duke pressed his head deep into the blue pillow. "Wonderful." He reached for the morphine drip button but the nurse intercepted it.

"We'll get you something else to manage the pain."

"It's called morphine, you twit."

"Duke," Cassandra said. The nurse shuffled out of the room and closed the door.

Duke shut his eyes and tried to think. A week ago he was able to see the scrim opening. He played a virtual reality game once during a bachelor party and felt it was similar but this world he was in felt so *real*. The fidelity, the people, the *feeling*, it was all real to him. The bachelor party game only gave him feeling in the nether regions. Duke felt his broken arm and leg. *Am I going insane?* The drugs felt real to him, too. His years of sobriety were a distant and frivolous memory, like a cigarette tossed out of a car window.

The man who appeared in the scrim opening wasn't of this world. That was the fact Duke held to. It was his fall that opened up the scrim. Something set a sensor askew. Duke felt ill for a moment. He realized the only way to reopen the scrim was to hurt himself again. If he could see the real world again and remove those cables, maybe it would be possible to escape this hell.

"Get me a wheelchair," Duke said.

"No, Duke. Look at yourself. You're strapped in. You have to just wait a few more days."

So much for a helpful partner. "Can you get me some coffee, at least? The good kind. Something not made in the same building where they cut people open."

Cassandra looked at him. "Okay." She tossed the magazine on the table next to the window. "Are you crying? What's wrong?"

Duke was afraid. Virtual world or not, this pain was real and what he was going to do might kill him. "I'm fine, just getting stir crazy."

Cassandra leaned over and kissed his head. "Don't you worry. I'll get you a glazed doughnut too. And when we get out of here I'm throwing you the biggest party you can imagine." She left the room.

About a year before Duke developed a hatred of hospitals, he spent summers in the green hills of Vermont. Rain or shine, he'd always end up swimming at the quarry. There were plenty of cliffs that surrounded the deep bluish-green water. Some were five feet high, but others towered to forty feet. Duke had always been big for his age. Even at five he towered over the other boys. Despite his size, his fear of plunging into the cold water from precipitous heights made him nearly wee himself. Duke would watch all of his friends leap off, giggling. Duke thought of the first time making the jump. *Old Man's Chin* is what the locals called it. Duke stood at the lip and tried seeing how far the stone stuck out in the water at the bottom. If he didn't jump out far enough he'd hit stone and break his legs. It was a humid summer day when he stood on the cliff's edge. His feet slipping against the smooth ancient stone. Duke went to the end of dirt path which had been packed down from years of use. He heard the calls from friends below, "Hulk! Hulk! Hulk!" A moniker he proudly wore.

Duke closed his eyes and breathed out the trepidation. "Jump far, one, two, three, jump far, one-two-three," he repeated to himself. Baby pine needles tickled his bare back as he stood amongst the brush. "Jump far, one-two," he ran, his knees pumping perpendicular to his hips, before he knew it, the edge had passed and he was airborne. "Jump fa—" Duke plunged toward the black abyss. The clouds blocked the sun and made it look like a void. Then he felt the chill of the mountain water caress his body. Duke had done it, but heights still terrified him. That's why he became a plumber. Most pipes don't run near the ledges of buildings or cliffs.

Birds twittered outside Duke's hospital room window. He tried to measure the height from where he lay, but found it futile. He prayed it was no higher than the third floor. That would certainly kill him. Duke grunted. "Jump far, one…" He yanked out his IVs. "Two-three…" The pain was a sharp sting, but nothing like what he was about to feel next. Grabbing hold of the catheter he felt the tube move deep within his groin. "Jump-far-one-two-three." He tugged out the catheter and wailed. It felt like he'd pulled his member inside out. *It's not real, it's not real.* He swung his good leg out of the bed and tried standing. Duke paused for a moment to breathe and settle the dizziness. Then he shimmied over to the window and looked down. *Fifth floor.* Now all of the alarms were going off. His vital sensors lay on the ground. The heart rate monitor flashed and beeped. He heard the nurses' footsteps coming from outside. "Jump far." Heaving the chair up with his good arm, he released it in the direction of the window. Glass shattered brilliantly across the linoleum floor. Duke was relieved to see an awning jutting out from the second floor onto a balcony. Instead of jumping far, he'd have to stick close to the building and hit that to break his fall. Duke kept repeating, "Jump far one-two-three," over and over, as if he were chanting monk. The jarring pain of his hip and newly-fused femur was shifting against new bone; like stone against stone.

Using his cast, Duke brushed away the glass on the bottom of the window. He sat on the ledge and faced the hospital door, unable to look at the heights below. He never tried scuba diving, but had seen how it was done before. A team of nurses swarmed into the hospital room and held a look of absolute terror.

"Easy now, Duke," the meek nurse said.

"What's going on?" said a distant voice that sounded like Cassandra. She rounded the corner and stood behind the frozen team of nurses. "DUKE!?"

They couldn't tell what the massive man was muttering. "Jump far, one-two-three, jump far, one-t—" Duke fell back with the perfect form of a seasoned diver. The fall was longer than the Vermont quarry. It was timeless. Flashes of black and white and red and blue. Duke crashed through the awning and clipped an air conditioner unit that bulged from an employee lounge. This sent him tomahawking. He tumbled head over heels until he landed in the high hedges that lined the first floor of the hospital. Ironically it was the side of the building that housed the morgue. For a moment he didn't move, but soon his lungs demanded oxygen, delivering strength to his shattered bones and torn flesh. White matter lay in the dirt. Duke soon realized it was the remnants of his left eye. He closed both eyes and ignored the agony while trying to focus.

Opening his one good eye he searched for the opening, but it wasn't there. He looked and couldn't see it, just the dirt and blood and matter that lay about. His casts had shattered and cotton blew amongst him in the breeze. Forcing himself to roll from his stomach to his back took several dizzying seconds. When he finally did, he realized his spine was a few inches off-centered and parts of his body felt like Jello and sand. He hadn't realized yet that his foot had been torn in two and was hanging only by his Achilles tendon. Duke reached out at the blue sky, searching for the opening, but only saw his hands. He wailed in pain and slammed his head against the ground. That's when he saw it. A tiny opening in the scrim of the blue sky was a hospital light. Duke stopped screaming and pounded his head again, this time with more force. The sky opened further. A hospital light, then the white fissured ceiling tiles, then more light. He struck his head again, this blow nearly causing him to black out. The scrim didn't grow. He tried again but there was no progress. Duke was growing weaker. He was dying.

"Over here," shouted a voice in the distance.

Duke knew he couldn't be saved. This was his only chance. He was so close. He turned his good eye to the ground and punched himself in the face three times. Agony speared through him like electric shocks. A couple of teeth swished around his mouth. The scrim opened entirely this time. He saw everything: the lab of floor seventy-two, the hospital bed his body lay in, the computer monitors. He saw Cole.

"There he is!" said a nurse. Duke could hear the footsteps running toward him and the sound of a stretcher's wheels trying to keep up with their pace. He heard Cassandra too.

Duke swung his hand beneath him into the dirt and ignored the resistance his brain set for him. His fingers brushed the cables in the real world. "Jump far," he muttered as he heaved again, this time getting a full grip. Duke yanked on the cable and the remaining scene of the virtual world, the outer walls of the hospital, the hedges, the blue sky, all became outlines against a white plain. The suffering no longer mattered to him. Duke had breached the chrysalis. He wrapped the cables around his hand and centered his grip. Duke noticed a mirror against the wall. It shimmered the reflection of a man coming into focus; the same man who had shut his world away. "Jump fa—" Duke drew the cables back and the virtual world, his own virtual hell of addiction and agony vanished like waking from a dream. It was gone. He breathed the fresh air of the real world again; his injuries were gone but the pain lingered with pins and needles.

Duke began pulling the IVs from his body again. He moaned when he saw there was a catheter in the real world too. Some things don't get easier the second time. Once he was free, a door opened behind him. Duke saw Leif holding a coffee with a look of stark terror. Duke lunged from the bed and grabbed his collar and belt and heaved the skinny man above his head and threw him across the room. Leif felt a moment of weightlessness, and then crashed into a silver medical cabinet. Duke grunted and yelled, following Leif's direction. He pulled Leif from the cabinets by his ankles and tossed him on the hospital bed. Leif moaned as he drifted in and out of consciousness. He wasn't a man of high fortitude. A paper cut would bother him for days. Leif heard Duke asking something, but it came out in muffled tones.

Duke, frustrated and riding high with adrenaline, looked at the man who'd been responsible for all his pain. He grabbed hold of Leif's wrist and elbow and bent it the opposite direction. A frazzle of cracks sounded and Leif's adrenaline instantly matched Duke's. He cried out and wouldn't stop until Duke held his mouth shut with his giant hands. He pinched Leif's nose to sufficiently sever all air from his body. Duke leaned down closely to the whimpering engineer.

"You'll suffocate in two minutes. I'll give you air back if you promise not to scream," Duke said calmly. Leif's eyes were as wide as saucers. He nodded furiously. Duke released and the engineer gasped for air, slurping it up like it was thick liquid. Leif glanced at his mangled arm and looked away.

"Where am I?" Duke asked.

"Jan—Janus Tow…the Janus Tow…"

"Janus Tower?"

Leif nodded, tears rolling down red cheeks.

"How do I get out of here?"

"You can't."

Duke held Leif's nose and mouth shut again. He squirmed and kicked and cried. After a full sixty seconds Duke released and Leif gasped for life again. "How do I get out of here?"

"It's a secure floor."

"How many others?"

"I monitor this lab but Ma—Mart—"

"Martin?"

Leif nodded. "He's running the show."

"Is he here now?"

"It's the middle of the night," Leif answered.

This stirred Duke. "What? It was just daytime."

Leif's eyes widened again as the pain began radiating up his arm and into his chest. "In *your world* it was. Time is diff—different here."

"How long have I been in this place?"

"A couple of days."

"Days? But not weeks?"

"No. Please, I—"

Duke held his throat and grunted into his ear, "You're going to pull my friend here out of his virtual world, and then you're getting us out of the tower. If not, this—" Duke flexed his fingers around Leif's larynx, "will leave your little neck." Leif cried but nodded. Duke helped the skinny man from the hospital bed. They walked over to tend to Cole, who was in the middle of riding down a country road with his father, enjoying a Coloradan sunset.

TWENTY TWO

Time felt different underground. It was easy to lose track of the passing hours. Saba checked her watch and noted that it had just crossed the four hour mark since they left the safehouse. Rafiq was doing a decent job at leading the team. He claimed they were in the tunnel he was familiar with. Saba shrugged. *Looks all the same to me.*

"Shouldn't be much longer," he said with relief. Rafiq never wanted to be put in this position; he hated leading. He'd always been fine with following an adequate leader or being on his own. The prospect of people depending on him gave him stomach cramps. Self-doubt was the nucleus of endless agony. Rafiq always thrived at looking out for number one: himself. He was sad about Duke and Cole being stuck in that weird future city; he vowed to help, so his conscience could be somewhat clear, but he didn't see himself having the dedication the three women had. Rafiq imagined helping for as long as he could, but eventually he'd pack up and leave. Maybe head west and see what work he could get in Oregon. He'd heard about how pretty it was over there.

"Does the door lock on the other side?" Eliza asked.

"What?" Rafiq said, squinting ahead in the darkness, still walking.

"The door underneath the Tollbooth Café, does it have a lock?"

Rafiq kept walking on the wet ground. He was trying to remember. "I don't think so."

Eliza humphed.

"I'll break the door down if it does," Rafiq said assuringly. "But it shouldn't be locked. Zelda wouldn't do that."

"You mean the girl who has been a ghost since Ainsley's video went live?"

Rafiq said nothing and walked on in silence.

* * *

As Saba's watch marked the fifth hour of their journey, Rafiq pointed his light at the door. They'd passed by a dozen doors in the last hour, but all of them seemed to be sealed like crypts. This one looked different; a unique patina had developed across its center. *Stripes?* Saba shined her light and the stripes disappeared. She held the light on an off angle from the door and watched the patina of stripes reappear. The door was similar to the others. It looked like it was taken from an old battleship: oval shaped, with external locking mechanisms jutting from all sides.

"Tollbooth," Rafiq said, acknowledging the stripes. "It's a pattern tollbooth gates used to have, before everything went digital."

"Nice touch," Saba said.

The team approached. Ainsley was the first to put her hand on the handle. "May I?" she asked.

Rafiq shrugged, but a rumble inside the tunnel stopped them all cold. The ground vibrated, and far away in the darkness low pings echoed off the walls. The team doused their lights and remained very still. A cold silence returned to the tunnel. Then the outer rims of the walls and ceiling began to light up. A series of blue and white light fixtures grew to life, starting from the far end of the tunnel. The light approached like a wave and passed the team in a blinding flash.

That's when they saw it. The silhouettes of men approaching from the other side of the tunnel. Ainsley pushed the handle of the door and it creaked open just inches apart. "C'mon," she said, but as she went to open the door further a series of red beams shot down the tunnel, causing the door to slam shut. Ainsley pushed the door again, but it was as if a new force held it closed. The red beam was continuous. Feeding from one end of the tunnel to the other.

"It's a magnet," Saba said. "Everyone, against the door."

The team pushed against the door as the guards' boots grew louder. The door opened slightly, then a bit more. They could see the darkness on the other side. Rafiq wedged his flashlight in the opening. He forced it against the magnetic force in between the door and wall, acting as a lever. "Go," he muttered. One by one the team slipped through the breach. Rafiq was last to go and that's when he noticed the flashlight bending. He rushed underneath the flashlight and through the door just as it gave in, causing the door to slam shut.

Saba turned on her flashlight. "Tell me there's a lock on this end, Rafiq."

Rafiq wiped sweat from his brow and nodded. He cranked the center wheel and watched metal bars shoot into the ground, ceiling and walls.

Everyone exhaled a sigh of relief.

"How they find us?" Rafiq asked.

"It was only a matter of time," Saba said.

Ainsley held a hand out forward. "Care to guide the final leg?"

Rafiq nodded. "Yeah, it's a little weird. It'll get narrower until it gets better."

The team made their way into the Tollbooth tunnel, Saba bringing up the rear. Eliza remarked they were now officially cut off from Crystalline. *I'll believe it when I'm above ground,* Saba thought. As they made their way through the tunnel they began to smell something alarming, a toxic and dead smell, like burnt hair. An aroma of bad coffee lingered. Rafiq was getting worried. He tried reasoning that this was what the sewer level smelled like, but it was no use.

They came out of the void that connected to the dead-end tunnel which Rafiq last led Duke and Cole around. Now they were in the innards of the café subbasement, the brick corridor which led them toward the basement. Rafiq didn't share with the team that there should be lighting in this corridor. Soon they were in the basement beside the bookcases of Zelda's library. No light was on in there, either. Rafiq guided the team up the stairs and was so startled he dropped his flashlight instantly.

"What is it?" Eliza asked.

"What's that smell?" Ainsley asked.

Saba shined the light on the basement door and whispered, "No."

Rafiq took Saba's flashlight and pointed it on the basement door. It was a smoldering heap of charred wood. The molding around the frame had melted. They ascended the stairs, the smell of burning decay growing omnipresent. Rafiq placed his hand on the door. It was warm. He pushed it slightly and the whole thing fell forward like a tombstone. What lay before them was the burning remains of the Tollbooth Café.

* * *

The team emerged from the shell-like structure of the basement and observed the skeletal remains of the café. Major sections of the roof had collapsed into itself and pushed the walls over like dominos. Some walls, which held rebar and concrete, stood like ruins from a time long ago. Occasional gusts of wind blew the scraps around the heap. The metal appliances didn't melt, and stood gleaming and covered in ash. Plinths of destruction, standing proud as if they had stories to tell. Horrifying stories.

The basement stairs led them into the backroom of the café where coffee beans and other kitchen items were kept. A winding metal staircase led to the second floor beside the commercial washing machine and stainless steel sink, both now holding a greenish-red patina. There was a wall separating this backroom from the coffee bar and cash register, but that had burned away. They could see to the other side of the building, beyond the espresso machine, beyond the charred tables and on to the broken glass windows. The front door was gone and yellow caution tape wrapped the entrance.

Rafiq was did a short stint as a volunteer firefighter when he was in high school. He used the firehouse mainly to workout or sneak girls in. After going to a three-alarm fire he knew this wasn't the career for him. Drawing from his limited expertise he could say confidently that the fire had started in the upstairs office. The front of the café was the most heavily cooked. The second floor had burned so intensely it simply was ash, which allowed the fire to gain more oxygen and burn through the roof, causing those remains to fall through the second floor and onto the tables and chairs of the first floor. There were bits of computer parts lying about too, along with clothes, ceramic mugs and plates.

Curious pigeons watched the man and three women move about the wreckage and then move outside to the ash laden sidewalk. They walked around confused, like a set of aliens who crash landed on a new planet. Saba pushed her hair back and adjusted her ponytail. Rafiq took out his phone and tried getting a signal. Ainsley was staring back at the skyline of the city she gave up everything for. From this distance the neon pinkish hue looked less vibrant, like seeing a photo of a lavender field that had been aged by the sun.

Rafiq dialed Zelda and it went straight to voicemail. He cursed and pocketed the phone.

"I'm sure she's fine," Eliza said.

"Doesn't look *fine*," Rafiq muttered. He walked away from the remains and sat on the curb, putting his feet over the small river that ran along the gutter. Debris had clogged the nearby storm drain.

"Do you think it was them?" Ainsley asked Saba.

"I don't know. Depends how it started. It would be unlike them to send their guys out of the city," Saba answered.

As they were speaking a gunmetal gray Audi station wagon pulled into one of the café parking spots, its yellow headlights lighting up the four downtrodden people. They moved away from the car cautiously. A lanky woman with jet-black hair climbed out of the car holding a thermos of coffee. She stared at the three women with suspicion, then she recognized the man at the curb.

"Rafiq?" she asked.

Rafiq looked up and held a look of shock. "Zelda!" He climbed up from the curb and headed to her car. They embraced. "I thought the worst, I—"

"Relax dude, I'm here. Those pricks got me good. Thankfully I'm insured," Zelda said with a sly grin. She looked over at the women and flicked her nose up. "You're Cole's sister, right?"

Ainsley walked over to Zelda. "I've been trying to contact you. We really—"

"Where's Cole?" Zelda asked. "Where's Gigantor?"

There was a moment of silence.

Saba spoke up. "They've been captured."

"God dammit, I told him to be careful, I told him—" Zelda stopped and collected her thoughts. "I've been offline for days. The night after I helped, excuse me, was fooled by you," Zelda pointed at Ainsley, "the Crystalline Cyber Protection Department unleashed a virus into my rig. The thing caught fire and nearly cooked me in the process."

Ainsley looked back at the charred remains of the building. "Jesus, I'm so sorry, I—"

"I'm sure you are. You're a fucking good luck charm. Your brother comes to help and gets captured, my café burns to the ground and then—"

Ainsley's fists clenched as she stared at Zelda.

"We can sit here and argue all day, but that won't change anything," Saba interrupted. "I'll ensure you are compensated for what happened here. We need your help. No tricks this time. We have no one else."

Zelda looked at Rafiq. "What do you think?"

"I think Cole needs you," Rafiq said. "Plus… don't you want to get back at those bastards?"

Zelda smirked and looked back at Saba. "Whatever number you had in mind, double it."

Saba scowled but nodded. "Fair enough."

"I need a new rig too, that I want you to pay for as well," Zelda said.

"Fine. Only if we can get out of here and someplace safe," Saba said.

"We can crash at my place. It ain't big but it'll do for now," Rafiq said.

"Alright, get in. I'll drive," Zelda said.

A moment later the gunmetal gray Audi veered out of sight from the remnants of the Tollbooth Café. The skyline of Crystalline faded in the distance.

TWENTY THREE

Courtney Shay was Cole's first girlfriend. He met her at a basement party when they were sixteen years old. They left the party after she laughed at Cole's *Star Wars* jokes. His Jar Jar Binks impression was flawless. They kissed for the first time that night. Over the course of a year they had many other firsts. Eventually they parted ways, but he dreamt of her for years after. The long strands of strawberry blonde hair, her perfectly imperfect smile, the way she snorted when she laughed, the curves of her hips. "Courtney Shay is *the one who got away…*" Cole used to whisper in the lonely morning light of his dorm room. He stopped checking her Janus profile to initiate the forgetting process. It started to work. The heartbreak went from a hot burning pain to a dull ache. That is, until she walked into the Billy Goat Diner one morning.

Cole wanted to check out his favorite hometown diner. He borrowed the family pickup truck and parked right outside the restaurant. A neon sign read: *Billy Goat Diner EST. 1932.* A taxidermal Billy Goat stood propped up on a set of rocks outside the converted train car. Cole ordered the Billy Waffles because of their fame. It was the same waffle iron they'd used since opening the diner a century ago. He was halfway through the blueberries and cream waffles when she walked in the door. Cole had his head down and was in the midst of trying to fit a crescent-shaped waffle into his mouth when he spotted her.

"Cole Wainwright?!" Courtney said as she hurried over to him at the counter.

Cole chewed quickly and swallowed. "Courtney! My God, it's been so long." He got up from his barstool and hugged her, strands of her strawberry hair stuck to his syrup speckled cheeks. He wiped his mouth and she sat beside him. "You still in Longmont?"

"Yep, I run a small stationary store around the block," she said, brushing her left hand through her hair, no wedding band in sight. Cole made a mental note. "What brings you to town? I figured you're too fancy for us country bumpkins now?" She smiled her imperfect smile. Cole smelled her perfume or shampoo, he could never tell, and became overwhelmed by the nostalgia. Coupled with three cups of coffee, he felt ecstatic.

"The usual, Courtney?" asked a waiter from behind the counter.

Courtney nodded and slid next to Cole on the plush red leather stools. "Mind if I join you?"

"Of course." Cole pushed aside his copy of *Wired* magazine.

Courtney poured sugar, a lot of it, into her cup and stirred. She flipped her hair to one side and smiled at Cole. They both peppered in their pasts between bites. Cole told her about his short time at college and his new gig near Crystalline. Courtney nodded and was infatuated with Cole's every word.

"Remember that night after prom?" Her smile now a sultry grin.

Cole's heart sped up as a flood of naked memories poured in. "How could I forget?"

"Well," Courtney sipped her mug, which somehow looked different…more white, so white it looked like it had been cut out of reality itself. "If you're free later we can go to the lake again." Courtney paused, but didn't speak again. She seemed to be frozen.

Cole noticed the pies in their glass cases shimmer and then morph to the bare outlines, their crusts reduced to bumpy lines and a tangled pattern, a series of squiggles illustrating where the raspberries once were. Through the window the Rockies had disappeared and it looked like they were in a flat state, like Kansas or Iowa. Cole began to feel warm, sweat beaded along his brow. Courtney hadn't moved. Coffee spilled out of her cup but didn't reach the ground, an Escher-like waterfall of brown liquid never striking the tile. The 1950s doo-wop music played at a lower RPM, making the entire scene feel like a nightmare. The waiter by the Bunn Coffee machine was staring at Cole, his eyes locked and full blue like two dead computer screens. The coffee spilling from the steel craft wasn't hitting the ground either. Then he was gone. Checkered nothingness replaced the image, a holding pattern in the scrim of reality, existence in limbo. Cole went to speak but found his voice was gone.

Things turned stranger from there. Everything, forks, pies, babies, began to disappear in rapid succession. His world began to decouple like space junk reentering the atmosphere. Soon it was Cole standing on an infinite white plain with pale outlines only there to denote the horizon and ground. He opened his mouth to scream and heard the tearing sound of audio waves pitch and woe as the plain grew brighter and whiter than he'd ever seen. Whiter than the sun on a cloudless midday.

Time paused. Another world began to animate itself, but in a familiar pattern, one as simple as opening your eyes several times after a long sleep. The concept of reality hit Cole hard. He sat up in a hospital bed and screamed. Looking around, his vision was blurry. Gunk had clogged his eyes from days of forced sleep. He rubbed them furiously and saw a strange skinny mannish boy with his arm in a sling pecking away on a glass tablet. Cole recognized the man next to him, but for a moment forgot his name. Then it came to him. "Duke?" he said as loud as his dry vocal cords would allow.

"Welcome back, buddy," Duke said. "Welcome back."

* * *

"It's too risky, I can't do it," said the voice on the phone.

"You'll be fine. You're outside the walls," Saba said as she twirled a pen in her hand, the speed increasing with her rage. "This story can make your career."

"If I had a dollar for every time I heard that—"

"So you're backing out?"

"Well…"

Saba threw the pen across Rafiq's apartment. "If you are, then let me know right now, because I need to speak with the others that have a spine."

"Oh fuc—"

Saba hung up the phone and grunted. "Well Jeeves Wilkinson, former *Times* reporter, who has close to three million subscribers is out."

"Shit. That's the fifth reporter today," Eliza said as she updated her records.

"I know," Saba said loudly. A tense silence lingered for awhile until Saba broke it with: "I'm going for a walk. Is there a bakery or something around here?" she asked Rafiq as she slipped on her black leather jacket.

"Uh yeah. There's a Dunkin Donuts two blocks north… you need company?" Rafiq said.

"No." Saba stormed out.

Rafiq looked back at Eliza and they both shrugged. The journalists that promised to cover the story of Crystalline had backed out in droves due to a mixture of fear for their own reputations and other miscellaneous reasons. Saba wondered if they were being paid off. Either way, morale was low.

Zelda and Ainsley were in the second bedroom, which Rafiq had converted into a home gym. They were assembling the Orion-Tau MK 51b, the latest and most expensive rig on the market. Zelda was practically salivating over the power it had while she was installing it. *I could run a space probe to Neptune with this thing.* As it powered on, all of the lights flickered in shades of amber and white; the liquid cooling systems were powering up. Ainsley proved to be helpful with the install. "It's intuitive enough," Ainsley commented.

Zelda smiled. "You certainly are related to Cole."

Ainsley smiled and dropped her head, hiding an approaching frown.

Zelda looked at her. "Hey, we'll get them home."

Ainsley nodded but said nothing.

The Orion-Tau pinged and beeped as it booted up. Zelda took off her sweater and tossed it on the weight rack. "I'll need some time to get situated with locating Cole and Duke. The Janus Tower is no easy feat. Practically impossible. Do you have a plan for what to do when you find them?"

"I'm hoping Cole will help. We need to find a way to speak with him. Maybe he could do some damage from the inside before they go."

"I think you've watched too many movies. When you're in a place like that, the only objective is to get out."

Ainsley nodded. "But he could help us open the gates, right? I mean he's *inside*."

"Yes, in theory. But we don't…"

"What?"

"We don't know what condition he'll be in. Who knows what these lunatics have done?"

Ainsley's eyes pooled slightly. "Well, if we don't find them… what are we going to do? I'm talking about Saba's, I mean *our* goal. Opening the gates, letting the people out, having their story told to the world."

Zelda was typing into her terminal screen and grinned. "We have a backdoor it seems. Your husband's Orion-Tau is still powered on in the apartment. I think I can—" Zelda struck a key and one of the four nearby screens powered on and showed the inside of a palatial office that was familiar to Ainsley.

"Is that Martin's office?"

"Yep. I was able to follow his data storage accounts from the home computer to the work computer. This is the built-in webcam on his screen."

"Where is he?" Ainsley asked. "He should be at his desk. He's pretty regimented."

"That's what worries me. Hang on, I'm looking at his activity logs from the last two days and there's barely any activity." Zelda went through the webcam logs during the active times and noticed a skinny guy appear in front of the computer. "You recognize him?" Zelda asked.

Ainsley looked at the man on the screen. He was rail thin, wearing a Janus hoody; the foam of the milk in his latte matched his ghostly pale skin. She squinted at the image and shook her head. "Nah, I've never seen him before."

* * *

The craving an alcoholic feels for a drink isn't like the craving for water when you're thirsty. It's a drive to *feel* the release that alcohol grants. The entire body craves the feeling and the subsequent mental clarity and euphoria that soon follows the second, third, and eventually sixth drink. The demons of the day seem to burrow down and go to sleep, but never die. They come back angrier, but that's for the following morning. When the demons haven't been put to sleep in awhile they get malicious and fuel an insatiable craving for the drink. When the alcoholic cannot get that drink, they start to experience withdrawal. Alcohol withdrawal can kill you. Heroin withdrawal, while still unpleasant, is arguably safer. The first outwardly visible signs of withdrawal from any substance is the same: shaking and sweating.

Duke had been sweating for the last hour. Although he'd broken his sobriety in a virtual environment, his brain, or at least parts of it, believed the experiences be true. The good news was that his physical body hadn't consumed any of the substances he abused in the virtual world, which meant he wasn't going to die from withdrawal. However, the placebo effect was taking its toll and manifesting itself physically in Duke. He tried convincing himself that the virtual environment wasn't real, but couldn't shake the feeling. The years of sobriety were as solid as smoke trails. When he cleaned himself up in the lab bathroom, he flushed his bronze coin down the toilet, watching the triangle with the Roman numerals tumble out of sight. *My A.A. Group will never believe this story.* He chuckled with shame to himself.

"How you doing in there?" Duke called out to the shower stall.

"Fine…" Cole said over the static of the shower. "Fine," he said again, this time to himself.

Cole had been quiet since being pulled from the virtual world. He seemed upset that he had left. Duke wondered if he was thrown into a similar virtual hell of his former life. Soon the shower shut off and Cole changed back into his clothes. Leif was tied up in the outer room that housed the hospital beds. He had tried making a run for it, but Duke had pulled him by the ear—so severely there would be permanent damage—back into the lab. Like a young colt that had been broken by a seasoned cowboy, Leif now knew his place in the world. He must obey his master.

Duke wiped the new shore of sweat that flowed from his scalp with a towel. "It's not real. It's not real. It's not—"

"What happened to you in there?" Cole asked as he dried his hair.

"I should ask you the same thing, man. Seems like you're longing to go back," Duke said.

"No," Cole lied.

Duke gave him a look.

"Fine. It was nice," Cole admitted. "I was back home in Colorado with my family. It was all so… serene."

"Lucky you," Duke said, patting his head with the sweat-soaked towel. "They flooded me with sirens and sphinxes and broke my sobriety."

"Is that why you're…"

"Yes," Duke said, his hand trembling. "When I find Martin I'm going to tear his balls off."

"I just want to get out of here. What do you know? Did that techie give you anything?" Cole said as he laced his shoes.

"We're in a secure lab inside the Janus Tower. On a high floor."

"Terrific. Well, if we can get to a computer I can try and call Ainsley or Rafiq."

Duke nodded, holding back a lump of vomit that gurgled beneath his tonsils. He closed his eyes and settled his stomach mentally by breathing slow and steady. Cole gave him time to collect himself. Ten minutes later they were back in front of Leif, who shuddered at the sight of Duke, although he somehow seemed weaker.

"Okay *Bushes*," Duke said as he kicked the man in the stomach, hoping to transfer some of his pain to Leif. "We need a computer with an outside connection."

Leif cried and nodded. "The observation room."

"Very good," Duke said as he untied Leif.

Cole followed Duke and Leif into the other room and they had him log into the system. Cole pushed Leif aside and began running a protocol to secure his transmission. It took time, but eventually he was able to ensure its fidelity.

"When's your boss back?" Duke grunted.

"I don't know. A few hours? He's with the council. He has to explain that everything is under control. That could take a long time."

Cole's eyebrow perked up. "He's talking to the higher ups? Are they in the building?"

"Top floor."

"Wonderful," Cole said. He took time to situate himself in the system with the intent of penetrating the tower's internals. Then he went back to trying Ainsley and Saba's phones. Both were dead. *Did they leave the city?* he wondered. Cole tried Rafiq and got no answer either. He tried again, and this time it picked up. "If this is the collection agency I told you pricks I'm not liable, it was her fault—"

"Rafiq!" Cole said.

"Cole? Holy shit."

"Where are you? Saba and Ainsley's phones are dead."

Duke continued to wipe sweat from his brow. He watched Cole as he spoke into the headset. He didn't need to know what Rafiq had said. The look of despair crept through Cole's face like an infection. They had left them.

TWENTY FOUR

"We had no choice, Cole," Ainsley said into the vid-screen. Saba stood behind her with her arms crossed. Zelda was off to the side editing and enhancing the algorithm Cole wrote to break through the tower's internals. Cole was upset, but saw the logic.

"Okay, okay. We'll try and move according to plan: open the gates, spread the message, let the people out to tell their story. How many journalists will be waiting?"

Saba cleared her throat. "Three."

"Three…?" Cole said at nearly a whisper.

"I'm trying to get more. But…"

"They think we're crackpots," Eliza said bluntly.

A silence lingered and a guttural noise sounded behind Cole. He turned and observed Duke. The man had lost all color and abandoned wiping his sweat. Beads clung against his scalp and ran down his forehead, flooding the horizontal lines like irrigation channels on a farm. Cole thought it would be foolish asking *how he was doing.*

"We need to get Duke out of Crystalline. He's decaying," Cole said, scowling at the wounded technician in the corner. Leif couldn't provide any help even if he wanted to. The closest thing that he'd worked on that resembled a human, albeit loosely, was his six-armed barista-bot. "If we can get into the tower's brain, I can open a path out of the building. But that still leaves us with the gates. We're about three miles from there. Any luck with them?"

Zelda shook her head. "It's a closed system. Completely closed and antiquated. I wouldn't be surprised if they ran that thing on weights and pulleys."

"Terrific. We're stuck in the tower. We have no way to get the people out of the city. Duke's dying. And no journalists care to share this."

"Ye of little faith…" Ainsley muttered.

Another uncomfortable silence filled both ends of the call. The guttural noises from Duke sounded worse. He had lay down and fell asleep, shaking.

"Hey, if none of this computer stuff works, we could use the equipment back at the job site," Rafiq said.

"What, and roll down that stretch of highway in a bulldozer at twenty miles an hour?" Cole said.

"Nah dude, the fuel truck. I'm thinking we set it on auto-pilot and… kaboom."

"That's not a bad idea, actually," Zelda said. "But how will the people get out around that mess?"

Rafiq shrugged. "Steal a fire truck too?"

Zelda laughed. "You need a ton of water to put out a fire that big. The last thing you'd want is the Crystalline side coming to put it out and wrangling all the citizens back in."

"We could use the drones," Cole said. "And gather sand from the riverbed shores."

Zelda stopped typing and considered this. "That would require a lot of sand. Maybe…" Zelda paused again, thinking, "we can use the drones to hit the gates. It won't be as clean as opening the damn gates, but it could be done. It would certainly be less messy than a fuel truck." Zelda said.

Cole nodded, "Can you—"

"Already working on it." Zelda said. "Eliza, we'll need your mapping expertise."

"On it. I'll send over what I have as soon as it's ready."

"Good. Cole, you're fine working alone to get out of the tower?" Zelda asked.

"I'm not sure how secure their internal system is yet. Leif's terminal is a good starting point. It's already cleared to go into plenty of different servers. I should be able to get what I need," Cole answered.

"Let's reconvene in two hours and see where we're at?" Zelda proposed. Everyone agreed, signed off, and felt a similar feeling they hadn't experienced in a long time: hope.

∗ ∗ ∗

Zelda opened up a terminal to locate the Stribog Mailer Drone system, which ran off of the Janus Network. The entire system of drones, close to ten thousand, all operated autonomously. This network took a decade of system modeling, beta-testing in the barren deserts of Nevada, and small pilot programs as Crystalline was being constructed. This made the drone network as old as the city, which, when compared to the age of other American cities wasn't much, but the unique factor was that the system had learned about every nook and cranny of the neon metropolis.

Tapping into the system's core, *the brain* as it were, would prove to be difficult, but not impossible. It had to have a central system for the drones to act symbiotically. If the external weather systems detected incoming high winds or lightning storms, they would all adjust accordingly. Stribog drones flew at rapid speeds throughout the city constantly. On the designated airspace highways they approached speeds of one-hundred and fifty miles per hour, though given the navigation of the city and occasional traffic build up they'd average a speed of one-hundred miles per hour. Ten-thousand drones all moving at an average speed of one-hundred miles per hour, nonstop, everyday, through ninety percent of weather meant the system's core had to be robust enough to track what were essentially ten-thousand swerving bullets. The system was truly a work of art and human ingenuity. But as with most computer code that helped better the lives of millions, it was taken for granted and expected to work flawlessly.

Zelda admired the work of the system. Personally, she felt upset that she was about to mangle parts of the code and eventually damage the hardware. It was akin to a bookmaker shoving a wrench into the Gutenberg printing press, or erasing the code inside Wozniak's prototypes. But Zelda knew it was the right thing to do. She was a gray hat hacker, but leaned heavily toward the lighter side. When she was a little girl with a small laptop, she wanted to build new things that helped humanity. As she aged out of her preteen years, she started to see that optimism doesn't always pay the bills. She soon became a hired gun for companies and thus entered the world of gray hat hacking, which really meant data gathering or behavior modification. She enjoyed corporate espionage because she was able to see into the minds of these brilliant engineers. Zelda had seen internal designs for products, systems and machines that only a handful of people in the world would see. She felt it wasn't entirely wrong, but just another arm of the capitalist world affecting the market.

Breaching a secure system starts by looking for insecure pathways into the code or backdoors. This was something the original engineers created to gain fast access to the system. Zelda was able to find one rather quickly, but had to still deploy her algorithm, which executed on tens of thousands of combinations of passwords each second. After an hour of letting the algorithm run and defending against approaching security protocols, she was in. Soon she was looking at the control module to the Stribog Mailer Drone system, a beautiful work of art that was built by human engineers, but perfected by the machine learning AI.

Now the fun began for Zelda. She had to fool the AI by producing a duplicated system and have it work on that. It was the old fashioned version of putting a looped security feed of an empty hallway. Zelda had her own program that could facilitate this.

Zelda tossed her head to the side to crack her neck. The program was now running. It would take awhile for it to write a working clone and make the switch. Lines of a self-scripting code reflected off her glasses. She drank some water and waited. Zelda hated waiting. It gives too much time for mistakes to brew.

TWENTY FIVE

Martin dropped two anti-nausea tablets into a tall glass of water and watched them fizz. He gulped it down despite the warning on the label. He craved relief from the sharp pains in his stomach. Stress, a feeling he could never shake, was coursing through him like oil through an engine. Speaking with the counsel of the societal government, the top people that effectively ran the city, exacerbated his stress to the point of a constant and unbearable pain.

"To conclude our meeting, I'll summarize and that should suffice for an abstract for the minute notes," the Chairman said, clearing his throat. "The actions taken by Ainsley Wainwright, the spouse of Martin Spiros, are punishable by immediate expulsion of Crystalline and a fine of $2.2 million for damages inflicted on the city, its citizens, and the business loss suffered to the Janus Corp. Mr. Spiros has agreed to lead the Crystalline Guard's search for Ainsley and her criminal conspirators…"

Martin finished his glass of water and grunted. He was waiting to hear the *or else* part of the Chairman's summary.

"…Failure to find the aforementioned criminals will result in Mr. Spiros's expulsion from Crystalline, a fine of $10.4 million, and banishment from the science and technology community."

The pain returned to his stomach. Anger helped him stay stoic. *That bitch.* Martin always sensed that Ainsley might cause problems, but never at this scale. He figured it would be on par with his colleagues' spouses: ennui, weight-gain, adultery…but not flat-out rebellion against the entire city. He took this job after graduating Stanford. *Silicon Valley is the heart of technology, but Crystalline will soon be the brain of it all, the leader in everything*, they said.

Ambition clouded his judgement and he jumped at the opportunity. Now he was paying the price. He was tasked to find his wife and discipline her. A tinge of sadness came across him, but he swallowed it. Martin didn't have a happy childhood. He learned from an early age that attachment to others is necessary, but can bring a man down forever. He imagined his heart as a Russian nesting doll. He'd open a few layers to others he felt intimacy towards, but never reveal the final shell. Ainsley had gotten the closest, but he still kept that final shell closed tight.

He licked the white sludge that moved slowly from the bottom of glass and thought of the next steps. Find Ainsley. Divorce. Sue her and the entire Wainwright family, then banish her from Crystalline. All would happen publicly to please the counsel and solidify her image as a lunatic. He could probably be remarried in two years. The first step was proving to be difficult though, but he had a chess piece he was willing to put in play: Cole. Martin smirked. Using Cole would be enough to draw her out from hiding.

He thanked the counsel and left the oval conference that sat at the pinnacle of the Janus Tower. Martin and his guards followed him to the elevator. Inside the chrome box, he tapped a button with the number seventy-two on it. The elevator shot down in a muffled hum. He licked his lips and noticed he was feeling much better. In fact, he felt ravenous.

∗ ∗ ∗

Leif sat in the corner holding his broken arm. The throbbing had intensified since Duke snapped it like a pencil. Thinking back a few hours ago to that event made him want to scream. He looked at the clock on the wall and tried to focus on seeing the minute hand move. This was a trick his dentist taught him—focus on the smallest of details and the body will forget the pain. Leif tried, but to no avail. The anxiety crept in with its incessant what-if scenarios: *what if my arm doesn't heal right?* He closed his eyes and pleaded silently for Martin to get there. Leif failed to mention that since the seditious videos put out by his wife and the assault on Dr. Geary, he'd been placed under protection by the Crystalline Guard. Leif prayed for Martin to show up with a tiny army, or enough to take down the Neanderthal that broke his arm.

Cole was hunched over the video screen talking to someone named Zelda. Duke seemed to be asleep, from the post-VR symptoms Leif guessed, but he didn't care. It would all be over soon enough. He started rocking back and forth while humming a tune his mother used to sing to him. It was an old nursery rhyme, but he forgot the words. Clutching his arm, he swayed back and forth in the corner. Soon the pain lessened and he began to smile. He fantasized about what environment he'd throw them both into. Perhaps their hell simulation. This made him giggle. Back and forth Leif gently moved; waiting. Back and forth, back and forth.

* * *

At a rest stop somewhere off I-80, Milo Doyle climbed into his eighteen-wheeler semitruck. He'd been driving for three days straight with the help of coffee, cocaine and beef jerky. Milo settled into the threadbare seat and stretched his arms forward against the glass of the windshield. A light rain had started to fall in dancing curtains. The veteran trucker let out a belch and started the big rig. He needed to stay on schedule. Rumors were hopping across the CB radios and roadside diners that these autonomous trucks were going to take their jobs. Most of the major shipping companies had already shifted their fleets to partially autonomous vessels and entirely autonomous warehouse staffers.

"Not today, fuckers," Milo said, thinking about *them damn robots* as he called them. He looked at his face in the side mirrors and poked the grey bags that sagged beneath his eyes. "You're beau-ti-ful," Milo chuckled as he pulled his lower lip off yellow teeth and packed in dipping tobacco. The big rig's RPMs settled and the diesel engine hummed smoothly. The trucker smiled and waved to a prostitute, who was limping toward the restrooms. He shifted into gear and drove back onto I-80. Eventually he made his way to the center lane of the highway and attained cruising speed. Milo tossed it into high gear and sat back, watching the rain dance off the green hood of his truck. Reaching over into a stained lunch bag, he pulled out a baloney, cheddar and mayo sandwich on rye. It was six days old. Halfway through the sandwich and washing it down with Mountain Dew he began to feel a wave of nausea overcome him.

"Oh boy," Milo said. He felt the sweat seeping atop his bald head. Shifting in his seat, he tried to pass gas, but couldn't. Milo's stomach began to bubble and churn. "Oh boy, oh boy." Opening the window, he tossed the sandwich out and tried breathing in the fresh farm air. He began to feel better and started laughing as he patted his belly. His ex-wives always said he had a raccoon's stomach.

Twenty miles later, the feeling returned. Violently. He began dry heaving and reached for a bucket in the passenger footwell. At seventy miles per hour, Milo Doyle vomited into the bucket. One hand on the wheel, the other on the center console. Waylon Jennings bellowed outlaw country over the retching. The big rig swerved across two lanes, nearly colliding with a minivan filled with schoolchildren. Car horns protested the great metal beast as it tore across the American blacktop. Eventually Milo saw blood in the bucket.

"Boy oh boy, fuck me," he cried out. Milo pulled himself up and tugged on the horn of the big rig. "Get out of here!" Milo tried pulling the truck out of gear, forgetting to depress the clutch. "Fuck!" Soon he recognized his error and downshifted the truck as he tapped the brakes. The truck slowed from seventy to fifty. He felt better, under control. As the ill trucker took a deep breath, he swallowed his dipping tobacco, gagged, and vomited once more against the windshield, blinding his field of vision.

Milo Doyle had been driving a truck his whole life. Throughout his travels he noted where those brake-failing ramps were likely to be. They were long stretches of road that were made for truckers in distress, who've lost control of their rigs. Milo could've sworn he saw the brake-fail ramp ahead and he turned the truck toward it, trying desperately to slow the rig. What he failed to recognize was he was still doing thirty miles an hour and rolling into a fuel station. The nausea, coupled with the sleep deprivation, brought on delirium. Milo felt he was doing a mere five miles an hour as he barreled onto the exit ramp. "Boy oh boy…" he mumbled.

* * *

Lawrence Henderson sat in the passenger seat of his car as fuel pumped into the tank. His notebook lay against the dash as he outlined the Crystalline story. *Is this what Ellsberg felt like in the 1970s, or Glenn Greenwald in 2012?* Lawrence smiled nervously. The information Saba Nazari had sent to him was shocking enough. But if he could get there in time for eyewitness accounts, that would make the story. He was just hours from the strange neon future city.

"Don't celebrate until it's in writing or the check is cashed," Lawrence said aloud, reciting the motto his first editor taught him. Lawrence smiled. He couldn't help himself. Surely this could be a book, perhaps a bestseller. He fantasized about the advance check these big publishers offer. "Amalfi, baby." Lawrence had always wanted to take his wife to the Italian coast. Finally, he'd be able to do it.

CLICK, thunk! The gas had topped off. Lawrence climbed out of the car and tried to squeeze out a few more drops to get the price to an even number. Looking back toward the entrance ramp, he noticed a green truck with bright headlights and a foggy yellow windshield rolling up the exit ramp toward the fuel station.

"Asshole better slow it down," Lawrence said as he returned the gas nozzle to its upright position. As he clicked the cap on the gas tank he noticed the truck hadn't slowed. "Fuck… FUCK!" Lawrence ran from his car and headed away from the gas pumps screaming. Other drivers ran, too. One woman held her nine month old as she ran into the station. Panic and terror rained down on this tiny gas station off I-80.

Milo had passed out and his big green Peterbilt plowed into the gas station as the trailer jackknifed off its hinge and rolled into the tanks. A high pitch piercing sounded a second before ignition. A flash of white. Then amber waves of flame rolled across the semi's trailer. Lawrence's freshly filled gas tank exploded, starting a chain reaction with the five other cars. Those who took cover in the station suffocated from the black smoke and soon burned. Lawrence had run past the station and tried making it to the parking lot, away from the carnage. A chunk of concrete struck the soon-to-be famous journalist in the back of the head, knocking him down. Lawrence staggered back to his feet as a tire from the Peterbilt truck was shot airborne from the explosion. It bounced twice, each in ten foot arcs, but then landed wheel side forward against Lawrence's skull, popping it open like a Medjool date.

The fire spread and cooked the gas station. It would be an hour before emergency responders arrived. Black smoke plumed into the blue sky, like soot against a new blouse. Somewhere a bird twittered as it flew by and headed toward the purple skyline that stood proudly against a hazy horizon.

TWENTY SIX

Zelda was in the final stages of bringing all of the drones under her control when she heard Saba swearing from the other room. Zelda cranked the volume on the McIntosh stereo system to drown her out. Schiller's deep electronic sounds coursed through the tiny room. A half hour passed and Zelda put the final touches on closing the loop between the Stribog system and her cloned system. The screens before her illustrated a matrix of mailer drones. It looked like a more complex version of air traffic control. Zelda now was the sole operator of Stribog Mailer Drones, all 10,546 of them. She celebrated silently with herself, as she often did in this business. Then she got up to treat herself to a victory beer.

She opened the door and passed by everyone with a coy smile. Tugging the fridge open, she reached in and grabbed a bottle. The bitter hoppy beer was cold and refreshing. Zelda smiled and looked out Rafiq's window at the drone traffic far in the distance; strands of green against the purple skyline. The setting sun was dying the earth gold, the shadows gray and soon black. Zelda flipped a middle finger at the Janus Tower, when she realized it was all very quiet. She made her way back to the living room where Rafiq, Ainsley, Eliza, and Saba were. Saba held her phone to the brim of her lips. She was muttering something in frantic spats. Saba looked up at Zelda, and then quickly looked away.

Ainsley turned around and saw Zelda. "It's Lawrence Henderson, our top journalist…"

"And…?"

"He's dead," Ainsley said.

"What? How?"

Saba shrugged and stared forward. "Freak accident."

No one spoke. Schiller's soothing electric synth sounds played from the speakers in the other room.

"We still have Aisha and Ansel," Ainsley said.

"Sounds like a Portland art gallery name," Zelda said with a smirk. She looked at Saba, who wasn't smiling. "Sorry, too soon," Zelda said sipping her beer. "Well, I have some good news. The drones are under my control. They're running their regular routes right now, but when you need me to take the helm, I'll be ready."

"Excellent. Excellent work, Zelda," Ainsley said.

Zelda nodded. "How's the route looking, Eliza?"

Eliza, who hadn't spoken in some time, looked up from her tablet with bloodshot eyes. "I modeled a variety of instances where the egress points were the main boulevards and thoroughfares, but it seems more effective if the people just flee west using all the streets. This will make it more difficult to contain. I've looked into these rising walls, and I think they're monitored from the Janus Tower. We'll have to make contingencies for what'll happen if we can't get control of them and they start to rise during the exodus."

"Good work," Zelda said checking her watch. "We'll be speaking with Cole in fifteen minutes. When are the two journalists expected?"

Saba, still looking forward in a thousand-yard stare, said, "Tomorrow morning."

"Good, that should give us plenty of time," Ainsley said reassuringly.

Saba looked at the floor. "Plenty of time too for more things to go wrong."

* * *

Cole hadn't moved from the desk. After Duke passed out and Leif went into a silent rocking state, the room became quiet and it felt like he was alone, in front of screens and a keyboard. He'd taken a similar path to Zelda in breaking into the mechanical unit of Janus and the subsequent parts of Crystalline that were vital for their escape. He produced a bot that could replicate itself and access the moveable walls that got them stuck there in the first place. A tinge of anger brewed for a moment when he realized this should've been reviewed by Ainsley and Saba *before* they decided to bring him over, but he let that feeling pass and focused on getting out.

Leaving the tower was another story. He could only get a partial view into some of the security cameras. This confused him. Either they didn't have them in certain parts of the building, which Cole felt was unlikely, or he wasn't looking in the right place. Cole figured an alternative route would be taking Leif's keycard and finding one for Duke so they could hustle out like regular employees. A problem with that was finding someone who matched Duke's physical description. Cole realized that taking the keycard was the only chance they had at this moment. He figured he should try every angle to get into the security feeds to aide their escape.

In his search for the security footage, Cole did learn more about floor seventy-two and the rest of the tower. It was built in modular blocks, similar to a space station. There were designated sections for specific work. Virtual reality and biological management of patients were all centered solely in room 11b, Duke and Cole being the previous occupants. Given the amount of technology for any given room, Cole saw the fire suppression systems were downright flawless. Halon systems produced clean agents to kill the fires, along with oxygen withdrawal ducts. During his stint at MIT, Cole lit three of his dorms on fire because he was running so many rigs at once. He smirked at the fire suppression system and thought that would've been a better use of their endowment funds than another eco-chic café.

Cole checked the time and called Zelda through his secure channel.

"Hey Cole," Zelda said. He saw the team behind her looking solemn.

"Hey Zel—" The buzz of the anterior door sounded and opened. Two chambers away Martin and four Crystalline Guards entered. They were separated by a long glass and steel corridor. Leif cackled with joy.

It took a moment for Martin to process who was sitting at the computer. When he did, a glare from fifty yards away made Cole freeze. The guards ran down the corridor toward him. Cole lunged from the desk to the door and locked it. Martin and the guards were midway down the corridor now. Cole kept an eye on the door they entered through, waiting in a starkly calm manner. Neither Martin nor the guards could see what Cole's hand was resting on as he watched them approach. Martin's shouts grew louder, sounding like an incessant beast. Then the rear door closed and Cole smiled. He pulled the red lever against the wall, which activated the fire alarm. A blaring alarm sounded and the corridor turned red. Auxiliary lighting lit the floors and soon the Halon system sprayed its clean agent against the four men. It looked like a space shuttle launchpad. Relentless layers of white smoke jettisoned from the ceiling ducts. Cole watched the screen beside the lever and saw the oxygen levels depleting.

It took much longer than Cole anticipated. They got to the office door and the guards attempted to break the glass with the butts of their pistols. After a mere minute, their rage had diminished. The men were starting to become aware of the lack of oxygen. It wasn't like the movies. The guards didn't demand the doors be opened. Instead, they retreated. Martin led the guards back the way they came. But it was too late. They collapsed one by one. Martin was the last to fall, with his hand against the lever of the door.

Cole returned to the computer and looked into the screen. "We need to leave. Right. Now."

TWENTY SEVEN

Ansel Sparks checked into his hotel, which was one-hundred miles from Crystalline. After unpacking and washing up, he returned downstairs to the lobby. The friendly concierge directed him to his table in the restaurant, a private booth set back in an alcove. There was a scotch, served neat, and a tall bottle of mineral water waiting for him. Ansel spread out his notebook and unfolded his laptop, ready to work his night shift.

He managed to finish his emails before the first scotch was finished. Ansel submitted his latest story on Avi Mizrah, the billionaire crypto currency magnate who joined the space race years ago. Ansel was tasked to cover the new printer prototypes that were being sent to the Moon's south pole. The mission was to print tented cities within the lunar craters and develop greenhouses. Ansel enjoyed his time with that subject, because he was more grounded than most billionaires he'd met. He was also happy because Avi had paid him handsomely and put him up at this hotel even after the story was complete.

An hour passed and the tuxedo-clad waiter took away his plate, which had the remnants of a steak dinner: discarded pieces of fat and sautéed spinach. Ansel smiled, wiped his mouth, and then returned to his work of outlining tomorrow's assignment: Crystalline. He reviewed the notes that Saba had sent him. They were scattered and difficult to follow. This soon made him uneasy. He'd dealt with a lot of crackpots in his tenure as an investigative journalist, which honed his bullshit meter to a finely tuned machine. The claims Saba was stating were extraordinary and warranted investigation. *How could a company get away this shit like this?* He smirked and answered his own question: *If there could be a company capable of this it would be Janus.*

After dessert, he wrapped up his outline and began to wonder if this story was going to have any legs at all. The same waiter returned and took an empty bowl which once contained chocolate mousse. Ansel left a generous tip and returned to his suite.

While he was reading an old McCullough biography, his phone pinged. It was an email from Avi. He opened it and his eyes widened as he read through the note. Avi was introducing his sister, Talia, who was the foremost naval architect in the world. She was best known for spending her entire career on building a city completely underwater. Ansel wondered if they were only allowed to read Jules Verne novels as children. Talia seldom spoke to the press, which made this opportunity tantalizing; the high pay was also a bonus. It would keep the bill collectors at bay for awhile.

A sentence stood out as a problem though: "I'm leaving tomorrow for Atlantis II. The jet leaves at noon. Would you care to accompany us?" This meant he'd have to abandon the Crystalline story. Ansel set down the phone and rubbed his temples. Then he made his decision.

* * *

The fire alarms stirred Duke awake. He could see through blurry vision the halon gases being shot through the corridor. It was something he didn't recognize and for a moment Duke believed he was back in the virtual world. Then he saw Cole run to the computer. He knew he wasn't in the virtual world when he heard Cole speak. "We need to leave. Right. Now." The voices spoke back. It sounded like Zelda.

"Patch me the feed you have, Cole; maybe I'll be able to operate the controls from here. It's a long shot, but let's try," Zelda said.

A tense silence hung as Cole and Zelda worked together. Duke managed to get up and stand steadily. His headache reduced to a low humming pain. He felt dehydrated and whelmed with strange aches and floating currents of nausea that passed through him like breeze through a wheat field. Duke exhaled slowly and managed to stand steadily for a few more moments until he spoke. "Cole," Duke said.

Cole's head turned around with concern. "Can you walk?"

Duke nodded, though it didn't fill Cole with much confidence.

"Alright, I'm in, albeit partially. I can only see chunks of the building. The kitchen and cafeteria area on floor four has an exit to the elevated walkway that wraps this district," Zelda said. "The work that you were doing on controlling the walls seems to be gone. We'll deal with that later."

"Got it. I'll speak to you through Leif's phone," Cole said. "Hey Duke, would you mind?" Cole motioned to Leif, who was cowering in the corner. Duke smiled. Leif didn't even resist. He fumbled for his phone in his lab coat pocket. Duke thanked Leif by faking a punch and making him shudder. Duke gave the phone to Cole. He worked for a few minutes on downloading a Tor program to the phone to delay tracking. Duke spent the time tying up Leif against the desk leg.

"See you on the other side, guys," Zelda said. Cole nodded and dialed Zelda. She gave a thumbs up on the vid screen, confirming the connection. "Let me know when you make it to the fourth floor."

"Will do," Cole said into the earpiece.

Duke unlocked the door and both of them descended town the corridor. They approached the unconscious guards slowly. They were breathing. Cole took two security badges from the guards. Then they stripped down the guards that anatomically matched them. Duke was surprised the jacket fit him, but didn't even bother with the guard's pants. They both took the belts from their respective guard, which held a Beretta U22 along with other utility tools such as mace, flashlights, a multitool, and the like.

Dressed as guards, they made their way down the corridor, past an unconscious Martin Spiros, and out of the lab of floor seventy-two. Duke closed the door behind them, locked it and grimaced.

"What?" Cole asked.

Duke said nothing. A throbbing vein grew from his neck and formed a *v* on the center of his forehead. The handle of the door he held bent and broke off. Cole gave an approving nod. The two entered the elevator and descended to the fourth floor.

TWENTY EIGHT

The elevator didn't feel as if it were moving. There was a low humming and ambient music playing softly. A moment later, the door pinged and opened onto floor four. Even though it was close to five o'clock in the morning, there were still plenty of employees milling about, getting early breakfast or finishing up their nightshift. They ignored Duke and Cole. The omnipresence of security guards in the building made them as common as trash receptacles. They walked into the cafeteria, which had Cherrywood tables, glass and chrome chairs. It looked like a futuristic dojo. They took a seat in the corner and dialed Zelda. The connection had severed when they were in the elevator.

"Hey, we're on floor four in the café," Cole said.

"Okay. The guards saw the alarms on floor seventy-two and have moved from their various posts and swarmed the lobby. This means the main and rear entrances are out. I suggest moving through the kitchen and taking the service elevator," Zelda said.

Cole considered this and asked her to send the lobby security feed to his phone. A moment later he was receiving snapshots of the ground floor. A total of three dozen guards and rising. "Let's walk out the front door," Cole said.

"What?" Duke said.

"Cole?" Zelda said.

"Look at it. The place is swarming with them; we're in uniform," Cole said. "We'll be able to blend in long enough to make it out of the building, then head for the gates."

No one spoke. Just the ambient conversations of other diners drifted through the air.

Zelda spoke first. "Well Cole, you do have a point. Keep your heads down and out of the camera's sightline. There's a service elevator that'll bring you to the lobby. Move your ass."

The duo got up quietly and moved through the kitchen, past tired cooks and janitors, and took the elevator. Moments later, the doors opened and a flurry of noise roared. It sounded like an old Wall Street trading floor. All employees were being held in organized lines and searched.

"C'mon, my boss said I can't be late to another morning meeting," one man said.

"There goes the 5:20 shuttle," a blonde haired woman muttered.

"He's cute," a young intern said as Duke walked by.

Cole and Duke moved at a steady pace through the crowds. It seemed every person who was trying to leave was being inspected. Outside, past the revolving doors, security guards patrolled the area. Red beams from security drones cast down like stage lights along the tower's perimeter. They hovered back and forth on the open space between the building and roadways; this caused Cole and Duke to slow.

"Keep moving, guys," Zelda said. "Northwest exit is your best bet. There's a traffic jam on that side of the street. Once you leave, ditch the hats and jackets and try to blend."

"Got it," Cole said.

They moved past the security guards. A strange kind of functional fear was operating Cole. He felt his adrenaline pumping into his arms and legs; his brain was shouting "Run!" Cole treated the situation like a well written line of code. He knew if all the variables he accounted for remained constant, they'd make it. They were halfway through the crowd when Zelda mumbled something.

"What was that?" Cole asked.

"Shit…its Martin," Zelda said.

Cole turned around and saw Martin exiting the main elevator, a medical team following him along with his guards. Duke moved faster through the crowd, parting the sea of people.

"Hey, watch it buddy," one guard said to Duke.

Duke moved faster. Cole followed suit; he knew this was wrong, but could no longer contain himself.

"Stop that tall guy!" a voice shouted from behind them. "Stop them!"

Duke exploded forward like a tight end at the start of a play—knocking over several security guards and two employees. Cole took out his mace and sprayed the men behind him. Duke leaned forward toward a guard with an uppercut and the man went down seizing. Alarms began to sound. They were only yards from the door. Cole noticed a drone was heading straight toward them with its searchlight pinned to the door.

"Take cover guys," Zelda said.

Duke and Cole immediately hit the ground, covering their heads. A flurry of drones, cascading off course, fell from the sky as they swarmed in a pattern toward the front of the tower. The first one missed but took out a guard with its rotors by severing his ankle. A half dozen more descended and exploded on the revolving door and windows. Fire, glass, smoke, and metal shot outward in all directions. The revolving door bent and melted under the high heat. Dozens of guards were killed or maimed.

A ringing sounded in Cole's ears, but he was conscious. The smoke burned in his nostrils. He looked over at Duke, who now had a severe nosebleed. They got to their feet and ran through the broken burning glass wall. Bullets ricocheted off the metal from the back of the building. A flurry of panicked employees and guards rioted through the lobby; some ran toward the elevators, others headed for the exit. Martin's screams were lost in the madness.

Duke and Cole made it to the street level and ditched their hats and jackets in a trashcan. "Where are we heading, Zelda?" Cole asked.

"I'm drawing a line. Look up," Zelda said.

Cole glanced at the night sky as he meandered through the sea of panicked pedestrians and noticed a line of green drones forming in a direction similar to a GPS route. The line of drones moved two blocks west and then bent north around a building. They followed, and after a few blocks the video screens and billboards that are fused on various buildings all shut off and rebooted with a familiar face: Ainsley Wainwright. She was broadcasting live from what looked like Rafiq's apartment. Saba stood beside her. They introduced themselves and continued the message of dissent. "Leave Crystalline. You've been lied to. The gates will be open by dawn. You're free to leave this prison. Follow the green line. Follow the drones. We will protect you. We need you to tell your story." The message was played on a continuous loop. Cole and Duke noticed something magical happening before them: the people were listening. One by one Crystalleans followed the beeline of drones toward the gates of the city.

TWENTY NINE

Aisha had been up for twenty hours straight trying to get to the outskirts of Crystalline. She had a meeting at noon with Saba and the rest of her team. Aisha had showered and eaten a microwaved cup of soup dinner in the motel bed. She tried watching something on the hotel TV but it seemed to be fixed to the Weather Channel. Aisha pulled off her jeans and crawled under the covers, which felt cool against her dark, slender legs. The red alarm clock read 5:25 am, enough time to get some rest. Slowly she drifted to sleep, listening to the rattling of the mini fridge and the windy lull of traffic spewing off I-80.

The beginnings of dreams were difficult to pinpoint. Aisha felt she was in a long library surrounded by yellowing books. A loud thumping bore out from the shelves. It was as if the books were alive. *Thump-thump-thump*. The large volumes: encyclopedias, atlases, and periodicals shuddered in place while smaller paperbacks fell off the shelves. A cold splash of fear made Aisha run, but the long shelved corridor stretched and stretched to an infinite horizon. Her feet slammed against the marble floors. More books fell and the ceiling overhead was the night sky; a smear of Milky Way shimmered brilliantly.

Aisha began to cry out something she hadn't heard since she was a little girl growing up in Chicago's south side: "No mama, don't go down there, don't go." It repeated and echoed between the vibrating books. At once all the books shot out of the shelves, striking Aisha. Her brow was cut and bloody, and so was her nose. She on running until a great globe fell in her way, causing her to fall. The books attacked her like hungry locusts, jettisoning from their perches and devouring. Aisha was soon covered in copies of leather-bound classics; Molière, Dumas and Béjart blocked her last line of sight to the night sky. Darkness fell. Her breathing began to labor and soon she suffocated. Right as she took her last gasp for life, she sprang up from the books, shooting them forward, and she watched them melt away and a dim motel room took its place. Covered in sweat, she looked around and noticed her nightmare wasn't over. Her door was ajar and four people were standing at the foot of her bed.

* * *

The message struck a chord with the Crystalleans. People sprang from their apartments in a mass exodus. Surely some loyalists remained, those afraid of the Crystalline Guard and tainting their resumes. Duke and Cole were now in a sea of people following the beeline the drones had set. The Crystalline Guard were scrambling from their posts, trying to contain those in their buildings. Some of the apartments, the more expensive ones like Pylône Sept, were hermetically sealed and locked; only three children managed to escape from the second floor balcony. One broke his leg and remained there. The shattering of windows added to the chaos. Occasional drones would dip from the beeline and collide with approaching scanner drones. The Stribog drones outnumbered the police a hundred to one.

The conglomerate of defectors were less than a mile from the gates when they felt the ground vibrate. A mechanical groan sounded throughout the streets and quieted the crowed. Some people stopped moving, afraid for what was next. Duke and Cole kept pushing through, making their way to the edge of the pack.

"Zelda, were you able to get into the walling systems?" Cole asked.

"Working on it," she answered, sounding stressed.

"We're going to need alternate routes set up. I can feel the ground starting to move."

"Working on it," she said again.

Cole and Duke pushed on, encouraging others to move with them as calmly as possible. They were at a high risk of being trampled to death by panic if the walls began to rise. Cole felt like a rat in a maze that was about to catch fire.

"Dammit, it's like they moved it. I cannot find the system anywhere," Zelda said.

Cole couldn't respond because a black wall began to rise behind him. Shouts and screams roared as the people scrambled to make it over the wall. Cars that were parked in the way were lifted in the air. One fell off the wall and crushed two young women. The crowd began to run. Duke held Cole close and pushed to the front of the pack. Nearly half of the exodus was blocked from following as the wall towered to fifteen feet high. As they ran, Cole noticed smaller walls rising in the alleyways, cutting off secondary and tertiary routes. The maze was set aflame.

They made it a couple of blocks when a great wall ahead of them slowly rose. They were too far away to make it over. Suddenly the drone beeline shifted and swayed left, pointing toward Janus Stadium. Its bright lights made it glow white against the purple skyline. "Follow it!" someone yelled. The Crystalleans moved fast through a narrow boulevard. Soon they were in sight of the stadium when a wall began to rise and split it in two.

"Zelda, the walls are now—"

"Get in the stadium. Head for the nosebleeds," Zelda said.

Drones from the beeline wavered off course and collided with the maintenance gate of Janus stadium. They ran straight onto the glorious football field and climbed into the stands. The wall stopped rising at forty feet. The nosebleed section was higher than eighty feet. One by one they climbed. Scanner drones began circling the stadium, but the Crystalleans disobeyed the commands and threats. Cole and Duke got to the precipice of the wall first and helped dozens of people over before moving on.

Cole looked out from the stadium and was able to see the gates. One by one drones circled the gates but didn't descend. Flashes from guard towers intermittently sprayed in the dawning light. Duke pushed Cole along. "No time Cole, we're not out of the woods yet." A dart shot by Duke's ear and struck an Asian man, who fell instantly between the stadium seats. Duke looked down at the field and watched a swarm of guards moving in. They were firing tranquilizer darts at the exodus. One by one people fell. Soon Cole and Duke made it into the stairwells, and minutes later exited they stadium. Ahead of them the beeline pointed toward a road which had walls, but only at three feet high, looking like tidal barriers.

"Zelda?" Cole started to speak.

"I found Market District's system. It's holding…for now," Zelda said, sounding exhausted. "You're close, Cole. You're very close."

* * *

Aisha stared at the group of people who had broken into her motel room, paralyzed in fear. Those Crystalline Guards that Saba had warned her about had found her. The rights that normally comforted her as a journalist weren't present. It wasn't until she saw Saba step into the light that the fear waned.

"What the hell is this?" Aisha said, pulling the covers over her naked mocha skin.

"We've been calling you. There's been a change of plans. The exodus is happening right now," Saba said. A man approached the bed holding her clothes.

"Get dressed. We'll explain on the way."

Aisha went to protest, but felt the graveness in Saba's voice. She complied, and as she pulled on her jeans she looked at the clock. "Fucking terrific," Aisha grumbled, seeing she only had an hour of sleep, most of it being fraught with nightmares.

Ten minutes later they were in an Audi station wagon speeding toward the purple skyline. A woman named Eliza sat next to her in the back of the car on a tablet, speaking to someone named Zelda and giving coordinates and cross streets.

"Where are the others?" Aisha asked Saba, who sat in the front seat beside Rafiq, who was driving.

"Lawrence is dead. Car accident," Saba answered.

Aisha sat back in horror. She'd known him well at the start of her career. He was a kind, honest man who helped her launch her own news site. "Accident?"

"I know what you're thinking, but we saw the security footage from the gas station where it happened. There's no way that could've been staged."

"Okay, okay… and how about Ansel?"

A silence lingered for too long.

Ainsley spoke. "Can't find him either. He hasn't returned our calls. I'm feeling he flaked on us."

"Jesus," Aisha said.

"You have your exclusive now, Aisha," Saba said, forcing a grin.

Aisha just kept looking out the window toward Crystalline and wondered if she were still dreaming.

<u>THIRTY</u>

The gates of Crystalline were vertical beams of iron and steel that stood forty-two feet high. Between the beams was a mesh that had an electric current running through it. The United States government contracted Janus to develop this type of wall along the southern border of Texas, Arizona, New Mexico, and California. With government funding, they were able to develop a perfect wall and gate. The gate, which was an impenetrable mixture of line-x and graphene, stood on a mechanical track and slid along the wall to open. The track was the weakest part of the entire wall. This was the target for the drones.

Cole and Duke were close now, with the other Crystalleans bringing up the rear. They had escaped Market District and entered Farmer's District, which mostly consisted of crop-lined fields and farms. But this stretch of road was desolate; nothing but small vegetation and dirt on both sides. No man's land. They all took cover at the last bastion of buildings and cars. Waiting for the beeline of drones to descend. But they didn't. Instead they were hovering in place. Sounding like a hornet's nest, the buzzing echoed between the buildings amongst the distant alarms.

"Sit tight, boys," Zelda said, anticipating their thoughts.

Two drones flew low along the road toward the gatehouse where a couple of guards had made a barrier. Zelda spoke through the PA system on the drones to the guards, but they were immediately shot at with wide black nets; the drones veered and then ascended to the sky.

"I'm trying to reason with these assholes," Zelda said. A few more minutes of warning did nothing. The guards stood fast. Zelda grunted and figured she'd have to give them more than a verbal warning. A cargo drone emerged from the southwest, near the Utility District. It was followed by ten more. They were holding barrels of fuel. One of the cargo drones flew toward the gatehouse at top speed. Bullets and nets were being launched at the drone, but they either missed or were intercepted by sacrificial drones. As the cargo drone was two hundred yards from the gatehouse a bullet scraped the barrel, causing a bit of fuel to leak onto the road. The drone veered away from the road and descended on the target. Some guards began to run from the gatehouse.

Forty yards from the gate the cargo drone crashed into the dirt before the gatehouse and exploded in a magnificent amber fireball; plumes of thick black smoke scraped the horizon as the conflagration spread. Small flames ate up the trail of leaked fuel. Still there was no movement from the gatehouse.

Zelda grunted into the phone and muttered something Cole couldn't understand. At once, all the stationary cargo drones moved forward toward the gates. A moment later the beeline of drones followed. The next two cargo drones were stopped by the cannon nets. They fell near the road; one exploded, and the other had a soft enough landing to where it leaked the fuel back into the earth. A collective sigh bore out from the Crystalleans.

The third drone was stopped.

Then the fourth.

That's when Cole turned around back toward the stadium. He could see the siren lights, and even make out a few guards back in the distance scaling the halted walls.

"Zelda, they're closing on us."

"Got it," Zelda said.

Soon a cargo drone doubled back and soared over their heads. It crashed before one of the low walls, setting the area ablaze. Cole breathed a bit of relief and watched a drone ahead of them veer by two of the nets and crash into the center of the gate. Everyone cheered, but when the wind moved the smoke away they could see the gate was still intact. Panic was now spreading; a hive mind of trapped people in stark danger.

The smoke filled the gatehouse and the guards ran out, exposed. This bought Zelda time to send three more drones onto the gate. More fire, more smoke. In the distance, they soon saw a group of white electric-SUVs speeding away from the gatehouse. The crowd moved forward, Cole leading the pack. One by one the drones fell against the gates. Duke was able to see a small chasm forming between the gate and wall.

"It's working," Duke said.

Cole remained silent and walked on. Two more drones fell and the gap widened.

"Holy hell, it's—"

"How are we supposed to get through that?" Cole said.

"Working on it," Zelda replied.

The last of the cargo drones fell and the gate widened into a fiery but extensive gap. The exodus was now fifty yards away, but couldn't get any closer. The heat was too much. "We can't wait for this to die down," a woman in a torn suit said.

The beeline of drones came into formation in a horizontal line that slowly descended. They all had a forty-five degree tilt; the buzzing echoed off the wall and increased to a deafening tone. As the drone line hovered yards from the ground, Cole smiled. Dirt began to shoot forward toward the flames. Soon the drones were just a yard above the ground, spewing waterfalls of dirt and rocks at the gate.

The blaze was fighting back, but soon became muddled; blooms of flames were able to sprout out, but the relentless force of dirt made it impossible to continue. The tower lights illuminated the black and gray smoke licking the walls of Crystalline. The drones ascended skyward again and raced back behind the exodus. They landed in a similar snakelike line and repeated the process of shooting dirt and rocks against the approaching guards. The drones moved back toward the city, keeping the guards at bay.

Cole stepped forward and led the others to the border. The area of the gate was still scorching; they all held their hands up, instinctively protecting themselves from the waves of heat. Bits of metal glowed red and orange like a satellite reentering the atmosphere. The dawn light made it difficult to see the flames that still lingered along the road and gatehouse roof. The hedges and flowers had been burned to their stems. They pressed on.

Through the gap, Cole noticed a set of headlights on the other side. Beyond that he saw the red and blue lights of fire trucks moving in the distance toward them. Cole watched the silhouettes of people exit the car. Now they were standing in front of the headlights and speaking to him. Cole couldn't hear exactly what they were saying over the commotion and burning sounds, but he recognized the voice of Ainsley. One by one they crossed the chasm out of Crystalline.

EPILOGUE

Cole looked through the oval window of the plane. It flew over farmland and rivers that looked like Earth's elder veins. Ainsley was next to him, reading a copy of *The New Yorker* which featured a black and white portrait of Aisha Kraus. Aisha's broke the Crystalline story on her website two weeks after the breach. It took her several days to sort through the first-hand interviews; they capped out at two-thousand and eight people. When they made it through the wall, some of the people fled and were never seen again. Others returned to the town outside the wall days later, wanting to give their story. Aisha was dedicated to getting the story right. When the story went live, Aisha's followers shared it with the rest of the world. From there it snowballed.

Media and law enforcement were calling for specifics. Aisha worked with Saba to help with correspondence. The following month, Ainsley and Saba were featured in *The New York Times*, *The Wall Street Journal*, *The New Yorker* and *The Washington Post*. The traditional media outlets from yesteryear still had sway and pushed the story around the world. Saba became the spokeswoman for the Crystalleans, with the goal of sharing their advancements in technology with the world.

The Janus Corporation distanced itself as best it could by stating a disgruntled faction of employees ruined their future city experiment. The board fired a slew of top officials, making Martin the fall guy. Janus eventually provided settlements to all the Crystalleans if they agreed to never speak of the city again; some took the money, others didn't. They surrendered the city to the United States government. Saba was in the process of converting Crystalline from a private entity to a township, so the public could live there.

Ainsley closed the magazine and looked at her brother. "Are we near the mountains yet?"

Cole shook his head and kept staring out the window. He was thinking of Duke, who had told him he was back at AA. He considered the virtual hell to be a true relapse; he was then a month sober.

Ainsley opened the magazine again and skimmed through to find the cartoons. "Well, let me know when you do. I haven't seen the Rockies in quite some time."

Cole nodded and then smiled, thinking of the virtual world he had been thrown into, granted against his will, and how he had yearned to see a Coloradan sunset ever since then. That was what pushed him through the horror that followed being pulled from the world. He didn't want to admit it, but he had been thinking about Colorado since the dust settled from Crystalline. He knew their lives wouldn't be the same from here on out. Ainsley wanted Cole to work with Zelda on proliferating the technology from Crystalline to the world. They both agreed it's the right thing to do. They'd start their work soon but he wanted to ground himself first. He needed a reset and craved something familiar, so he called his parents. They were thrilled that both their children would be visiting.

Awhile later, white capped mountains grew into sight. The green and brown pastures stopped at the foothills, and suddenly towering giants scraped across the earth. Sharp mounds, impossibly high, looked like exposed bone from the Jurassic period. He could see the teal and slate colored rivers sluice between the canyons. Peach clouds blanketed sections of the range, adding to its majesty. In the distance, off the tip of the wing, a storm grew in one of the valleys. It reminded him of the song that played in the virtual world, that John Denver tune. Cole hummed it softly as he watched America unfold forever. The country would never be the same again. The sheer amount of data and advanced tech is enough to spawn another industrial revolution.

Cole tapped his sister's shoulder. "Switch seats with me. There's something you have to see."

March 19, 2018; Truckee, California
January 2, 2019; Seattle, Washington

ACKNOWLEDGEMENTS

As with any thank you letter I'll try and keep it brief, I can already hear the Awards show playoff music now. First, and she will always be first to thank, is my fiancé Ashley Rose. She helped me burn my boats and fully commit to being a writer. More importantly, she reviews the storylines herself and urges me to do better. Next are my parents who lined their home with books and art. Without them I'd be uncultured and unable to see the wonder that hides in plain sight. My twin brother John opened my eyes to a level of cinema most film students seldom get to. He showed me the intricacies of Kubrick's *2001: A Space Odyssey* when we were 11.

Next, I have to thank my dear friend Eftychis, who believed in my art and saw the worlds I was trying to create when they were mere sketches and notes.

The vibrancy of the book would not exist without the incredibly striking work from the artist Beeple, also known as Mike Winkelmann. He's been creating original artwork every single day for the last decade. I'd been a fan for years and when I first started writing the book I felt the world of Crystalline had a common element. The cyberpunk future feel came alive gloriously and meshed well with the story. Mike was very generous in letting me use his work; I will be forever grateful. All of Mike's art can be seen here: www.beeple-crap.com.

The printing of this book would not be possible without my Typesetters. I cannot thank them enough for pre-ordering copies of the book in November 2018. These early sales made it possible to fund the first round of printing and also support other initiatives for the book's launch. To the names listed on the following page, thank you.

Typesetters

Adam Roenfeldt
Alex Rosales
Ainsley Woolridge
Amie Johnson
Amy Jamison
Amy Moroz
Ashley Rose Stumbaugh
Brent Hoagland
Christopher Smilios
Corey Eiges & Bri Eiges
Damien & Lauren Sorresso
Eftychis Mourginakis & Risa Mourginakis
Erin Otto
Gleb & Laura
Ginger Woolridge
Jeremia Maldonado & Chelsea Bikowski
John Francis Maisano
Kara & Bryan Schapperle
Katrine Stumbaugh

Kurt Stumbaugh
Laura Casale & Thomas Maisano
Luci Cro & Brownie
Maris Stentz McAleer
Matt Schwartz
Melissa Stumbaugh
Michael Miller
Omar Eltorai
Patrick Schweighart
Phil & Kristen
Robbie Ray
Robert Casale
Seth Borko
Stacy & Barry
Sy Hak
Theofani Baktidy
Trevor Wysocki
Tricia & Joe
Wendigo Wiedemann
William Fisher

ABOUT THE AUTHOR

Robert Maisano is the founder of Biplane Media, an organization that supports creatives who make stunning content which does more than simply entertain. He writes hard science-fiction that peers into the future we're about to enter. Robert has written several novellas and short stories as well as non-fiction articles. He's written for *Business Insider* and *Thought Catalog*. Currently, he lives in Seattle, Washington.

Read more stories at www.robertmaisano.com

CITATIONS & NOTES

Works Cited from Preface

† Coldewey, Devin. 2018. "18 new details about Elon Musk's re-designed, moon-bound 'Big F*ing Rocket'." *TechCrunch.* Oath Tech Network. September 19. https://techcrunch.com/2018/09/19/18-new-details-about-elon-musks-redesigned-moon-bound-big-fing-rocket/

‡ Coyne, Sarah M., Laura M. Padilla-Walker, Hailey G. Holmgren, and Laura A. Stockdale. 2018. "Instagrowth: A Longitudinal Growth Mixture Model of Social Media Time Use Across Adolescence." *Journal of Research on Adolescence*

§ Duff, Alistair S. 2016. "Rating the revolution: Silicon Valley in normative perspective." *Information, Communication & Society* 19 (11)

The author wishes to highlight the printing company, Lightning Source, and their commitment to environmental sustainability.

Lightning Source doesn't print in bulk like traditional publishers. Instead they use Print On Demand (POD) technology to fulfill only the orders placed. To continue their commitment to sustainability Lightning Source receives these certifications:

Forest Stewardship Council® (FSC®) The FSC® Council is a non-profit organization, promoting the environmentally appropriate, socially beneficial and economically viable management of the world's forests.
Sustainable Forestry Initiative® (SFI®) The Sustainable Forestry Initiative is an independent, internationally recognized non-profit organization responsible for the SFI certification standard, the world's largest single forest certification standard.
Programme for the Endorsement of Forest Certification™ (PEFC™) The PEFC™ Council is an independent, non-profit, non-governmental organization which promotes sustainability-managed forests through independent third-party certification.

Learn more about their commitment here:
https://www.ingramcontent.com/publishers/resources/environmental-responsibility

CPSIA information can be obtained
at www.ICGtesting.com
Printed in the USA
BVHW052357300119
539100BV00004B/6/P